SLAVES TO THE METAL HORDE

By
MILTON LESSER

I0541458

ARMCHAIR FICTION
PO Box 4369, Medford, Oregon 97501-0168

*For more information about Armchair Books and products, visit our
website at…*

www.armchairfiction.com

Or email us at…

armchairfiction@yahoo.com

WHEN ROBOTS WERE MAN'S MASTERS

Johnny Hope knew that Earth's vast robot armies had been initially created to serve humanity. Unfortunately for mankind, a terrible war and a great plague had all but destroyed civilization everywhere around the globe. This left many of the surviving pockets of humanity as slaves to the metal creatures they had once lorded over. And though he was filled with great confidence and the spirit of youth, the odds of Johnny Hope ever getting mankind back to its supremacy over its former metal servants seemed very remote at best…

Here is another engaging science fiction thriller from one of the most underrated—and certainly one of the most prolific—science fiction authors of the 1950s, Milton Lesser.

FOR A COMPLETE SECOND NOVEL, TURN TO PAGE 85

CAST OF CHARACTERS

JOHNNY HOPE

He lived in a small community that was free of plague and free of robot intervention—but not for long.

DIANE

She was a "Shining One," a survivor of the plague. But she was forever destined to carry the horrible disease.

HARRY STARBUCK

He was a muscle-bound, full-of-himself opportunist whose ambitions might well be disastrous to the future of Earth.

DeREGGIO

It's tough to cast into exile the son of a friend, but that's what this mayor of one of Earth's last free settlements had to do.

AMOS WESTLER

Not really the revolutionary type, yet he felt sure he could find the knowledge man needed to bring the rule of the robots to an end.

KELEHER

As the leader of surviving plague victims, it was his job to organize raids on non-plague villages, including Johnny Hope's.

CHAPTER ONE

JOHNNY Hope backed off warily, retreating toward the sun-dried creek bed, a jagged brown scar across the parched grassland. He carried no weapon and as the others closed in about him in a tightening semi-circle his eyes darted furtively in all directions. But all the faces were stamped, as from a mold, with uncompromising hostility.

Johnny licked his lips and said, "I want to bury them. Let me bury them and then I'll go. I promise."

DeReggio, the mayor, brandished his club—which was an old rifle stock with half the jagged, corroded barrel forming a handle. "Go," he said. He took a long stride toward Johnny, then changed his mind when the youth held his ground. "They cannot be buried, Johnny. You know your parents must be burned as the law dictates."

Blinking sweat from his eyes, Johnny felt the sun scorching down through the glaring midsummer heat-haze. "It was the last wish of my father," he said softly, his voice hardly more than a whisper. "That I should take them forth from the village and bury them with a prayer for their Christian souls."

"No!" DeReggio bellowed. He was a great-chested man with sloping shoulders and almost no neck. "We cannot deliver their bodies to you. We cannot let you come back into Hamilton Village and take them, for you comforted them in their last hours and are therefore a victim of the Plague yourself." He pointed with the rifle stock toward the far hills, purple with distance. "Go."

Johnny shook his head, planting his feet firmly, wiping sweat-dampened hands on the worn fabric of his denim trousers. Then he held his palms up and said, "Where? Where is the Plague?"

"You've been contaminated."

Nearly the entire village had gathered behind their mayor

5

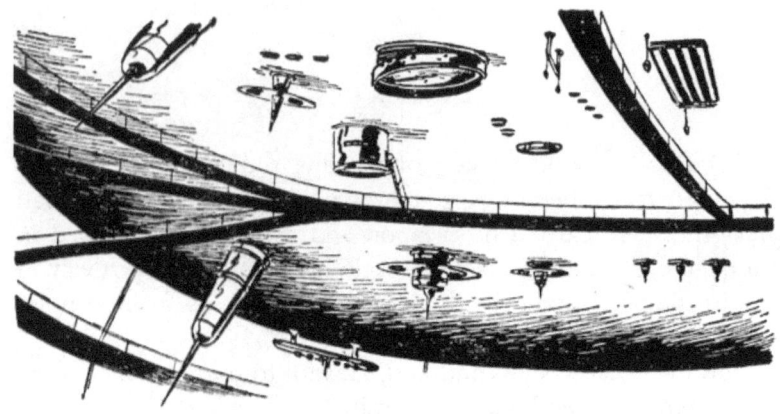

**Johnny Hope knew the robot armies had
been created to serve Man. But war and a plague
had destroyed civilization, leaving humans as —**

Slaves To The Metal Horde

by

Milton Lesser

now, and the mutterings were angry. When Johnny began to
walk toward them, his hands outstretched to show no plague
scars marked their skin, someone hurled a stone. Instinctively,
Johnny hunched his shoulder and caught the missile on his
collarbone. It jarred him and left an angry red mark where the
capillaries had burst beneath the skin.

Staggering back toward the creek bed, Johnny was felled by a
fusillade of stones. He crouched on all fours at the edge of the
dry brown earth, head spinning, vision blurring with pain. He
expected more stones to usher in the final blackness, but when
he could again see clearly, DeReggio's muscle-corded legs
straddled him and the mayor cried, "Enough! Let Johnny Hope
depart with his life." It was a brave gesture DeReggio had
made, approaching within inches of Johnny, whose parents had

been slain by the Plague. But DeReggio and Johnny's father had been close friends all their lives and had fought together in the last days of World War III before the Plague brought warfare—and civilization—to an abrupt halt.

Johnny forced himself upright on trembling legs. "I thank you for my life," he said, "but not for how you treat your dead companion-in-arms."

The color drained from DeReggio's olive-skinned face. "Think what you will, Johnny. Think it, but go while you still can. And remember that our first concern is with the living. The dead are beyond recall and the Plague victims can spread carnage in their wake. You know I loved your father like a brother, and your mother…"

DeReggio and Johnny's dead mother were cousins. They had been raised together under the same roof in the long-gone days before the War. Except for Johnny himself, the death of his parents could have disturbed no one more than DeReggio.

"All right," said Johnny. "I'll go." There was a loud sucking in of breaths—relief—from the crowd. "But first I have this to say. I have visited the old, ruined cities. I have seen Philadelphia on its river and once I went north as far as New York, the great stumps of its buildings coming right down to the water's edge on the island called Manhattan. I have seen these things and although I am young I tell you this: we will not return to our greatness unless we strike out boldly instead of sitting, huddled in fear, at the thought of the Plague."

"It is what his father always said," someone whispered from the edge of the crowd.

"The Robots will cure the Plague," someone else, a woman, declared.

Johnny laughed and had never heard such a sound before, from his lips or any others. "The Robots will cure nothing," he said. "Has anyone here ever seen the Robots?"

The faltering wave of sound from the crowd was in the negative.

"I have seen them," Johnny told his people, with whom he could no longer live. "My father wanted it that way. He sent me to the cities and to the mysterious places between the cities, the gleaming, white-surfaced roads that we use no longer, to see the Robots. And I tell you this: they will not cure the Plague. If anything they'll spread it."

A HUSHED silence fell, like a pall, on the assembly. None of them had ever seen the Robots, but that was because it is not proper for a mortal to see a deity. "This was the truth my father could not tell you in his lifetime," Johnny went on. "He knew you would have laughed and mocked—or worse. In his death I tell it to you for him. Along with his wish to be interred in the ground, it was his final thought."

DeReggio did not look Johnny squarely in the eye. "I think you had better go, lad. You have no right to talk like that."

Johnny shrugged, feeling the weight of a knowledge and wisdom beyond his years. "I am twenty-three," he said. "I was an infant when the War ended. Yet my father could teach me certain things and other things I could see for myself because he taught me to be curious and take nothing for granted. You could learn the same. Someday, perhaps…"

"By the Robots!" DeReggio swore softly, hissing the words almost in Johnny's ears. "Go before you antagonize them. If they start throwing things again, I won't be able to save you."

Johnny turned his back and squared his shoulders in a gesture compounded as much of defiance as contempt. He told DeReggio, "At least do one thing for me."

"If I can."

"When they are burned, say a prayer. One of the old prayers, if you remember." Johnny did not wait for an answer. He set forth—in long strides, his sandal-shod feet powdering the sunbaked ridges on the dry creek bed. He did not once look back over his shoulder, but now, with the people gone and his pride no longer a barrier, he sobbed softly, thinking of his parents who had died because they had to venture forth from Hamilton Village to learn some of the truths that were hidden from their people, and so they had come down with the Plague. Hours later, as the sun sank toward the western horizon and the heat of the day became less intense, Johnny heard the distant baying of dogs as the village hounds picked up his spoor and followed it. As prescribed by law, Mayor DeReggio was making certain Johnny did not double back to Hamilton Village.

He was alone in a hostile world that, in twenty years, had seen civilization come tumbling down like a house of cards in a hurricane.

THAT night, he slept uneasily on the bare ground, the soft-footed padding of foraging animals all around him under the dark moonless sky. He awoke with a tremendous hunger and a parching thirst. The latter he slaked in a swift-gushing stream that flowed clean and cool even in the heat of midsummer. Presently he came upon a huge black hawk, its pinions flapping, its talons sunk into the flesh of a dead cottontail rabbit as it prepared to fly off. Johnny waved his arms and shouted, frightening the bird of prey that rose without its breakfast, circled uncertainly, and then wheeled off to the east, a soaring black ghost graceful as a feather.

Johnny built a fire with brush and dry twigs and ate his meal in silence, feeling like a scavenger. He drank again from the stream and began to fashion himself a spear by uprooting a sapling and ripping off its branches and rubbing its tapering top to a fine point on the edge of a small flat boulder. He hardened the point in the embers of his dying fire, hefted the makeshift weapon experimentally, and headed north in the general direction of New York.

Two days later the joints of his knees and elbows began to stiffen. It came upon him slowly and he thought it was from too much walking and not enough food, but when the stiffness spread to ankles, wrist and neck and giddiness struck him suddenly, he began to suspect the Plague.

It was early afternoon and he sat down at the base of a thick-trunked oak tree, propping himself against the bole. He hurled his useless spear away and wondered how long it would take before he sank into the final coma and death. He ran swollen fingers across his knees and realized they had puffed to twice their normal size. He could now feel nothing from his knees down, and it was an effort to move his hands. A faint purple color suffused his limbs and any doubt he may have harbored about the Plague vanished.

DeReggio was right. Johnny tried to rise and failed, rolling over helplessly to lie half in and half out of the cooling shade shed by the oak. The chills rushed up from his feet, and engulfed him, followed at once by fever. By the time he began mumbling in delirium, the sun was going down in the west, casting long red cloud fingers into the darkening sky.

CHAPTER TWO

DIANE darted from the stream with a glad little cry, shaking the water from her long, tawny hair, the droplets of water sparkling on her bronzed skin like diamonds, the long, lithe lines of her body clothed only in the moisture until she found her buckskin shorts and halter and dressed. Life was comparatively simple and uncomplicated among the Shining Ones, and she, of all their encampment, remembered no other way. The others might look back with bitter longing or curse softly and futilely at the silver patches of skin at elbow and knee which marked them as survivors of the Plague, but not Diane.

So what if they were shunned by others, by the non-afflicted people who clung so doggedly to their mean existence in the small villages? She had but to hunt and fish and evade the bands of roving Robots lest they conscript her in their services. The only other bane in her life was Harry Starbuck and she could take care of herself where he was concerned. She could— and she would.

Something stirred in the undergrowth to her left and Diane could barely make out the flash of skin that said it was a man and not an animal. She finished fastening her halter as if she had seen or heard nothing, then abruptly picked up her hunting knife and said, "I hear you in there. I'll count three and then come in after you."

She did not have to count. The bushes parted and Harry Starbuck emerged, his skin scratched by brambles, his boyish face ridiculously out of place atop an over-muscled body, his knees and elbows covered by buckskin guards, an affectation common among the Shining Ones, but which Diane had always thought as silly as wearing eye patches because you did not like the color of your eyes.

"You were watching me," Diane said angrily. "I warned you before, Harry."

"There's no law, he boomed sullenly, his deep voice belonging to the over-developed body and not the boyish face. "I can go where I want to."

Diane slapped the flat of her knife against her palm slowly. "Someday, she predicted, "this blade is going to feast on Starbuck. I mean that."

Starbuck roared his laughter. "Then I'll be careful," he promised. "But meanwhile, you realize you can't marry anyone but a Shining One, and who of our people suits you more than…"

"None of them suit me."

"You're young. You have no family, no close friends to protect you. I should take you…"

Diane shrugged, then regretted it as Starbuck's small eyes feasted hungrily on the smooth play of muscle beneath the taut, bronzed skin. "Then go ahead, Harry. But you won't sleep nights, because I'll be waiting and if you do sleep you can forget all about waking up. I mean that, too."

Starbuck was still laughing. "I've half a mind to turn you over to the Robots and let them tame you a little before I claim what I want."

Diane let her voice do the shrugging. "You can always try."

"Must we always argue?" Starbuck demanded abruptly, petulance drawing down the corners of his lips. "I don't want to fight with you. I want to…"

"I know what you want. You can forget about it. I'm going to take a walk and maybe do some hunting. If you'll excuse me."

"With a knife."

"I'm not hunting for wild horses."

"I think I'll go with you."

Diane scowled at him, then girdled her knife. "As you wish, but be quiet."

Grinning, Starbuck shortened his strides and matched her pace as she cut away from the stream and the undergrowth and headed toward the foothills of the Pocono Mountains in the distance, where plump, juicy rabbits hid behind every clump of grass.

THEY walked in silence, the man's steps ponderous, the girl's so quick and lithe her bare feet hardly seemed to touch the ground. In an hour they had reached another stream, wider than the first and running deep with swift, cool water. Diane immediately dived in and swam, then continued walking on the other side while Starbuck carefully searched out a ford and splashed across with the water up to his waist. By the time he overtook Diane she was crouching, sitting on her bare heels, the line of her back, damp under the buckskins, a long, graceful curve.

"Take a look at this," she said, and pointed.

Starbuck looked and saw the remains of a campfire at her feet. "Warm?" he asked.

Diane shook her head. "But not completely cold. Several hours old. Probably made this morning. There's probably someone nearby."

"So what?"

"So if he's alone he's probably a Shining One and..."

"We have enough people in our camp now."

"You always think competitively, Harry. One more man won't hurt your position in our tribe."

"Well, if he's young and if he...well, if you..."

"I'm not promised to you or anyone, and don't forget that. Besides, it doesn't have a thing to do with this." Diane peered expertly at the ground and soon picked up the stranger's spoor where he had come out of the stream himself—probably after bathing—and started out on his day's journey.

"Come on," she said and Starbuck could either forgo her company or follow her.

He followed.

The spoor became erratic. It wandered in circles, doubled back on itself, seemed either headed for no goal or incapable of reaching one. "He must have been hurt somehow," Diane mused. "He can't be very far."

"What are you so curious about?"

"Curious? I don't know. I'm just interested. I—Hello! Up there—"

Diane sprinted up a short rise, leaving a surprised Starbuck pounding along several paces behind her. She found the man lying, face down near a large oak tree. Although it was comparatively cool, his body was drenched with perspiration. Diane shook her head sadly at the swollen joints and purple discolorations.

"They say it's a terrible thing," she told Starbuck as he panted up. "I don't remember; I was a baby."

Starbuck shuddered. "I remember. Watch out, don't go near him."

"What's the matter with you? We're immune."

Starbuck nodded morosely. "Yes. Immune. But he'll die anyway, so why don't we…"

"Why don't we take him back with us, that's what. Don't kid me, Harry Starbuck. You're acting sympathetic only because you think I'll like that. Well, I happen to feel sorry for this man. I think we'll feel better if we help him."

"Help him? He's as good as dead."

"Are you dead? You had the Plague. Am I?"

"No, but maybe one out of a hundred live. That isn't much of a chance for him."

"It's a chance, though. Here, carry him."

"What? Who, me? Now listen, Diane…"

Maybe a moon-struck Starbuck had his advantages. "Suit yourself, but don't expect me to speak to you again, ever."

Starbuck considered this, then mumbled something under his

breath that Diane couldn't hear. "All right," he said finally. "But I'm telling you it's a waste of time."

"I'll be the judge of that."

STILL grumbling, Starbuck picked the man up by one arm and one leg, staggered until he balanced his burden across one shoulder, then started back down toward the stream.

"That's right," said Diane. "We could reach camp in a few hours if we hurry."

"He'll never live through the day," said Starbuck. "I only had the Plague a few years ago, I lived in the villages, so I know. He'll never live through the day."

"Just keep walking. If he dies, we can bury him."

By the time they reached the stream again, Starbuck was covered with sweat. He forded the water carefully, Diane behind him to keep the stricken man's head above water. Despite its fever-flush, she liked the man's face. He was young, not much older than Diane herself, with dark hair and regular features, neither too boyish like Starbuck's, nor too craggy like most of the older men she knew.

Occasionally the man would mutter something unintelligible, and when they got to the other side of the stream he opened his eyes, stared at Diane without seeing her and said in a croaking whisper, "Water."

They stopped. Starbuck dropped his burden thankfully. "I can't carry him all the way back," he said.

"Then don't. Go ahead. I'll stay here." Diane cupped some water in her hand, trickled it between the dry lips. She was not even aware of Starbuck when he left.

She made a bed of leaves for the man's head and studied him. The denim trousers suggested village life, but she never suspected otherwise. The face still appealed to her, strong in appearance despite the fever, yet not overbearing. She hoped the youth would recover. "This is fantastic," Diane said aloud. "It may take days before he recovers…or dies." She thought of calling to Starbuck before he retreated beyond earshot, but her pride forbade that.

Shrugging and making herself as comfortable as she could, she bathed the man's flushed face with water.

DAY and night, the touch of the ground, the cool water that bathed him, the patient hands that kept the blood flowing through his swollen joints—all became as unreal to Johnny Hope as the shadowy remembrance of some half-forgotten nightmare. His lucid moments were few. There was this person, face unseen but comforting; there was a little food and all the water he wanted; and there was the fever that came and departed, leaving an icy chill behind.

Once Johnny mumbled, "Go away. You'll catch it yourself." And there was laughter, soft—murmuring, feminine, he thought. Was the woman insane to expose herself so?

The fever retreated stubbornly, in no great hurry to depart. The lucid moments became more frequent and of longer duration. The girl was beautiful.

There came a time when Johnny sat up weakly, his back propped against the bole of a tree. The face smiled at him. He willed the toes of his left foot to move and watched them wiggle. He could just barely feel them.

With long, easy strokes, the girl massaged his legs. Acutely conscious of her now, Johnny was embarrassed. "I'm all right," he said. He struggled to sit up but as yet had no real control over his limbs.

The girl placed the flat of her palm against his chest and pushed gently, easing him back against the tree. "You stay still," she told him. "You'll be up and around in a day or so, but don't hurry things."

"I ought to thank you. You're crazy. Why did you expose yourself like this? Why…"

He watched her as she sat before him and drew her legs up, knees thrust up. He saw the slim bronzed line of her calves and the metallic silver of knees.

"A Shining One!" he cried, recoiling involuntarily. The Shining Ones had survived the Plague, but remained carriers of it for all their days.

The girl smiled at him. "As are you. You're a very lucky young man to live through this."

The silver coated his own knees, Johnny saw, and his elbows. It would take some adjustment. All his life he had been told to walk in fear of the Shining Ones, who often swept down on the villages, forcing the townsfolk to flee or face the Plague, and taking what they wanted of the stores of food and supplies.

"I see you're a little afraid of yourself. It's common enough. I was lucky to have the Plague as an infant. I remember no other life, you see. When you're well and strong enough to walk, I'll take you back to our encampment."

"I don't know," Johnny said doubtfully.

"Just be patient with yourself. Adjustment will come."

"All my life they said the Shining Ones were monsters. When I was a little boy I had to be good because my mother said otherwise the Shining Ones would come and get me, carrying me off to kill me with the Plague."

"You've had the Plague yourself. You've got to remember that. Besides," the girl laughed easily, "you're too big a boy now to believe in boogey men."

"Well," Johnny continued stubbornly, "there are other things. The Shining Ones are scavengers. They don't work themselves or grow their own crops. Instead they invade the peaceful villages. Then the natives, my people, have to flee or become contaminated. The Shining Ones take all the loot they want."

"Only some of us. I have been a Shining One all my life and have never taken part in such a raid. We do not grow crops because we are not an agricultural people. We are nomadic and hunters."

"Why?"

"The Robots," the girl told him. "Some of our people join them voluntarily, many others are forced into bondage. If we don't keep on the move, they'll find us. Agriculture is an impossible art when your encampment is always on the move."

It gave Johnny food for thought, and something of the girl's own frankness made him do his thinking aloud. "If I remain alone, I'll be a hermit. I've seen the hermit Shining Ones wandering through the hills, alone and friendless, wild men. If I go with you, I become almost an enemy of my own people."

"They are no longer your people. You must realize that."

"And if I go with you, I can learn about the Robots and perhaps one day bring the truth back to my people. Tell me, do the Robots cure the Plague or spread it?"

"They spread it."

Johnny smiled grimly. "I will go with you."

TWO days and half a dozen good meals later, the girl helped him to his feet and nursed him along for his first few uncertain steps. But strength flowed back into his legs rapidly. He was walking without support by the time they reached the wide stream and saw the girl's nod of silent approval as he swam across it with her, matching swift stroke for stroke.

An hour went by and Johnny became amazed at the speed of his recovery. He almost wanted to return to Hamilton Village and shout, "See? I survived. I'm back." But he was a Shining One, a carrier, forever an exile from the people and the life he knew. And his own parents were dead, mute testimony of the havoc he might wreak among his people if he returned to them.

They walked from the stream and shook the water from themselves and looked at each other, wet like that, and smiled. "I don't even know your name," said Johnny.

"It's Diane."

"I'm Johnny Hope. I want to—"

"Johnny! Get down!"

He stood there, surprised, staring foolishly. They were on a small rise of ground above the stream. The girl, who had fallen flat even as she hissed the command at him, was tugging at his legs. He dropped prone beside her, although he still failed to see the reason for her sudden alarm. She parted the undergrowth in front of them with her hands and said the one word, "Look."

Johnny had never seen the Robots this close before. For all their ungainly bulk they trod the ground softly, walking as he had always seen them at greater distances, in a long, single file column. They were huge antenna-topped creatures, their great cylindrical head sections bigger than a man and gleaming a polished silver-blue, their eyes, four of them evenly spaced around the cylinder a foot or so below the antenna, white and bulging, with neither pupil nor lid, their limbs many-jointed and metallic, various tool-ends fastened securely instead of hands. The legs were attached to the small body, but one-fifth the size of the head; the arms came from the head itself, just below the unblinking eyes.

"They must be twelve feet tall," Johnny whispered.

"Shh! Softly. We're close to our encampment and I don't want them to find us. They average twelve feet in height."

JOHNNY would never forget the sight. Many times he had watched the robots parading in thin-lined silence down the long, silent roads that men no longer used, but now he could have almost reached out and touched them. The absolute quiet was unnerving. The Robots must have weighed close to a ton each but walked with the stillness of stalking jungle cats.

"Where are they going, Diane?"

"I don't know. Who understands the ways of Robots? Who can say…" Abruptly, Diane was still. Her eyes went big and wide but she wasn't watching the Robots.

Directly in front of her face and staring at her from unblinking eyes, its body half-coiled and dappled with the sunlight that filtered down through the foliage, was a copperhead. The tongue darted out in a quick, blurring red streak, the head cleared the loose coils and swayed slightly from side to side.

"Don't move," Johnny barely formed the words with his lips and hoped Diane would retain her presence of mind and obey him. A sudden motion would set the snake to striking.

The file of robots paraded by just in front of them, an occasional joint creaking, metal skins polished to keen reflection. The copperhead was fully coiled now, head cocked flat and ugly and perfectly still. Johnny placed his hand on Diane's thigh and let it crawl upwards, as if of its own volition, with an agonizing lack of speed. Now his fingers had reached the edge of the buckskin shorts and now they climbed on the smooth pelt. He could feel Diane trembling faintly, the motion unseen but felt. And now his fingers climbed to the girdling belt, grasped the handle of the hunting knife, and slowly withdrew it—tiny fractions of an inch at a time.

At last he had drawn the knife clear, easing it slowly toward his own body. He balanced it on his palm, trying to judge the weight. He would have only one chance, for the quick motion of his arm would make the copperhead strike if he missed. Sweat rolled down his forehead and into his eyes, half blinding him. He cursed soundlessly, held his hand out flat, squinted, whipped it forward. A sigh escaped Diane's lips.

There was an angry thrashing as the copperhead uncoiled. But the blade had pinned it to the ground, piercing the body just below the flat head. Ignoring the column of Robots now, Johnny crawled forward swiftly, grasped the knife and drew it cleanly toward him. The head was severed from the body. The body thrashed furiously, then lay still in death. The Robots marched on, oblivious of the drama that had unfolded at their metal-clawed feet.

The last Robot glided by, the long line retreated into the woodland, vanished.

Diane stood up, still trembling.

"It took me three days to save your life," she said. "You saved mine in seconds."

Johnny handed her the knife. "Let's find your people," he said.

CHAPTER THREE

IT was Harry Starbuck who met them when they emerged from a long, winding defile overgrown with vegetation. The defile opened into a depression, perhaps half a mile wide, surrounded on all sides by low hills, steep-sloped and blue green with pine. Unless the Robots happened upon the almost hidden defile, Diane's Shining Ones could not have selected a better hiding place for their present encampment.

Starbuck greeted Diane with, "In this case you had more luck than brains. I see he has survived."

"He's one of us now."

When she said that, Johnny looked down at his silver knees self-consciously. In time, he hoped, he would grow accustomed to it. But right now he felt himself somehow between two worlds, divorced from his own people but not ready to accept the nomadic existence of the Shining Ones.

Starbuck grinned without humor. "Well, then he's in time to help us move, although I'm opposed to it."

"To what?" Diane demanded angrily. "To Johnny? That's just too bad."

"Will you let me finish? Not to Johnny, if that's his name. To the move. Keleher has decided we have to move because a band of Robots trooped through earlier today. Maybe you saw them."

"We certainly did," Diane informed him.

"Well, I don't like it. Every time the Robots pass we have to start all over. What's so bad about the Robots anyway? They never bother us, do they?"

"They would conscript us, whether we liked it or not."

"Well, what of it? Rumor has it the conscriptees live like kings anyhow. We've got nothing to fear from the Robots."

"That's a matter of opinion, Harry," Diane replied.

At that moment, another man joined them. Johnny hardly had time to realize that he did not like the man named Harry. The newcomer was a big man, bigger than DeReggio, with huge shoulders almost three feet across and a long mane of graying hair almost reaching them. He wore a beard, spade-shaped and also gray, and covered his legs not with the expected buckskin but with khaki trousers he had probably stolen from one of the villages.

He greeted Diane briefly, then said, "Starbuck here told me how you were going to nurse a Plague victim back to health. Is this the man?"

Diane nodded and Keleher stuck out a powerful hand that Johnny pumped vigorously. "Glad to have you with us, son. In time you'll learn we're not the monsters you were led to believe all your life. But mark me—you owe your allegiance to us henceforth—provided you decide to stay." Johnny did not have to be introduced. Starbuck had mentioned a man named Keleher as their leader, and the newcomer spoke not with the bluster and arrogance of a leader unsure of his position, but with the calm self-assurance of a respected and powerful chieftain. Keleher would make a first-rate friend but a terrible enemy.

"He'll stay," Diane spoke for Johnny. "He doesn't look like a hermit, does he?"

"Never can tell. Where are you from, son?"

"Hamilton Village."

Keleher's smile was wry, almost rueful. "Will you put in with us?"

"I guess so."

Keleher shrugged, then took Diane aside and whispered to her. After that the big man turned and walked away. Diane was quiet.

"What's the matter?" Johnny wanted to know. "Does he always smile like that?"

"No, Johnny."

"Then tell me."

"We're going to leave this area because of the Robots.

Starbuck already told you that. We're going to travel light but we're still going to restock some of our supplies for the journey."

"I still don't see—"

"I don't know how to tell you this. The nearest village is Hamilton."

"So?"

"So we're going to raid it. We're going to raid your village, Johnny."

STARBUCK'S laughter carried through the entire encampment of conical tents, each flying its clan-standard from the central ridgepole.

Johnny wanted to hit the man, then realized he would be striking out at his own mixed up emotions. Diane was staring at him with genuine sympathy, but that hardly helped. She said, "What are you going to do, Johnny?"

"I'm not sure yet. I have to think."

"Remember, you're one of us now. Any time you doubt that, look at your knees or elbows. You are a Shining One, make no mistake."

"Yes, a Shining One." But Hamilton Village had been his home.

"We don't harm anyone," Diane explained. "I told you I take no part in the raids. I don't know why, for they're harmless."

"I saw one once, when I was a young boy. Before my people came to Hamilton Village to build their homes. The Shining Ones came down from the hills and simply walked into the village. There was no resistance. Our sentries gave us warning, but it hardly helped. We packed what we could and fled, leaving most of our supplies and equipment behind, leaving an entire village that we had called home but that we could never see again. The Shining Ones contaminate."

"Yes—we do," said Diane. "You do, too. The villagers can't fight us. We could walk down there unarmed and take what we want. Maybe that's why I prefer to hunt instead. I'm not sure, Johnny. What are you going to do?" She took his hand impulsively in hers and squeezed it. They hardly knew each other but they had saved each other's life.

"I wish I knew." He withdrew his hand awkwardly. He liked Diane, perhaps too much. But until he made up his mind she was a potential enemy.

Soon Keleher returned to them, not alone this time. A dozen men crowded behind him and others were leaving the tents of the various clans to join them. "Did you tell me his name?" Keleher asked Diane.

"No. He's Johnny Hope."

"Well, Hope, get a good meal under your belt and we're off. We leave for Hamilton Village later this afternoon. You ought to be able to tell us exactly where to find whatever we want once we get there."

Could a man change his allegiance overnight because he now was different physically? Johnny's heart was still in Hamilton, even if he had been stoned from the Village and his parents had been burned, as prescribed by law. But the rest of his life he would be a Shining One.

For a time he watched while Diane fixed his venison dinner, savoring the rich, gamey aroma. Then he slipped silently from the encampment.

OFTEN DeReggio would come to the large boulder half a mile north of Hamilton Village and sun himself contentedly, forgetting for the time at least the problems of his office. This rock was no secret. Any villager, not finding DeReggio in Hamilton itself, would know where to look for him.

Now he had almost drifted off into slumber. He always found this half-awake time most pleasant for dreaming. Then he could conjure visions of the old days, of the lost cities with the beat of their traffic pulse and the winking kaleidoscope of their electric lights, and the driving madness of their people that kept them seething with activity around the clock. He never traveled to the deserted cities himself as youngsters like Johnny Hope did, because their crumbling masonry and bomb-scarred streets saddened him. And besides, the Robots had taken over many of the cities and since no one had ever bothered to tabulate them, you were never sure when a city was deserted and when it was not. Better to dream of the old days...

"DeReggio! Wake up."

It was Sheldon Hope, his old comrade-in-arms, who had fought halfway across a world with him while civilization crumbled to ruin all about them.

"Shel...Shel, boy."

"Wake up, DeReggio. It's Johnny."

DeReggio sat bolt-upright, circles of light floating on blackness before his eyes from too much sun. "Johnny! Go away. They'll kill you if they find you here. Are you crazy? Keep away from me." DeReggio stood up and backed off, watching Johnny. "You have no business coming here. You—"

DeReggio saw the shining knees, the silver elbows. "The Plague. You survived it. You're a—"

"Shining One," Johnny finished for him as the mayor's voice trailed off.

"A carrier, that's even worse."

"I was hoping I would find you here. I knew I couldn't go down into Hamilton. You haven't much time."

"What are you talking about?"

"Shining Ones," Johnny said quickly. "Hundreds of them coming to raid Hamilton Village. They are on their way now. You'll have to leave, but I thought if I warned you, you could have some time to take your belongings."

DeREGGIO accepted the fact without question but with sadness. He shook his head from side to side, thinking of the neatly laid out streets, the small, compact bungalows, the field planted with hay for the cattle, with grain, asparagus, beans and tall corn waving green in the summer sun, ready for harvest.

"How much time do we have?"

"Four or five hours, I think."

"We'll have to hurry." DeReggio was already trotting back down the trail toward Hamilton, Johnny maintaining the pace with him but hanging back half a dozen long strides.

"I want to see the village once more, then I'll go."

"What are you going to do?"

"I don't know. The Shining Ones want me to stay with them, but I had to warn you. If they find out..."

"For my people, I thank you, Johnny."

First person plural. My people. Johnny no longer was included. If the Shining Ones discovered his treachery, he would indeed be homeless. He wondered what Diane would think.

"Look at the Village and then go, Johnny. If they find you, I won't be able to do a thing. And I wanted to tell you, I said the prayer for your mom and dad."

A figure appeared on the path up ahead. As he came closer the man's face was familiar, but his name eluded Johnny. "Mayor DeReggio!" he called. "I wanted to tell you my wife thinks..." His voice trailed off. He scuffed his feet in the dust of the path and squinted. "Johnny Hope!" he cried. "By the Robots, keep away. I have a wife and children."

"I only wanted to see Hamilton once more."

"We don't care what you wanted."

"He brought a warning," Mayor DeReggio explained. "The Shining ones are coming."

The man held his distance, but spat on the ground in disgust. "Look at him? You heed his warning? Look. He's a Shining One himself. It's some kind of a, trick you've fallen for."

DeReggio shrugged hopelessly. "You'll have to go Johnny."

Already the man was sprinting back down the path toward Hamilton. "I'll bring some of my friends," he called back over his shoulder. "We'll see about this. We'll see if a damned Shining One can go parading around Hamilton Village any time he wants. And you've got some explaining to do, DeReggio."

Then the man was gone. DeReggio turned to Johnny, almost shaking hands with him from force of habit, then drawing away in self-conscious confusion. "Good luck, boy. We'll be moving, despite what Lawford said. Don't try to follow us."

"I hope I haven't got you into any trouble."

"It won't be the first time."

"Thanks for the prayer. They would have liked that."

When DeReggio looked up, Johnny had vanished into the woods.

STARBUCK led one party of Shining Ones toward Hamilton from the north while Keleher took the main band in from the east. They never reached the Village though. Each leader saw the black pall of smoke rising long before he reached Hamilton. Each knew the Village had been put to the torch.

They met on high ground northeast of the flaming town and watched the fire, fanned by a strong summer wind, burn itself to embers and leave the charred skeleton of a village behind it.

"They got word," Starbuck said, waiting for Keleher to draw his own I conclusions.

"It's happened before, but now has anybody seen the new man, Johnny Hope?"

None of their followers had even heard of him.

"Diane would know," Starbuck suggested.

"She rarely joins our raiding parties." And Keleher checked, but as he suspected, Diane was not present. "Well, we move on empty handed. Starbuck, you take your men back to the encampment and round up stragglers or anyone who remained behind. We'll wait here."

"You're as bad as the people of Hamilton. Always on the run. I don't mean to argue, but—"

"Then don't. Men who want to be conscripted by the Robots are free to leave our encampment at any time, get that straight. But I don't want forced conscription of all of us, Starbuck. Understand? The Robots are around."

"Well, I was just letting you know how I felt. What about

Johnny Hope?"

"Time enough to see about him later, if he's still with the encampment. Naturally, if he's guilty he won't go unpunished."

"*If* he's guilty?"

"That's what I said."

"You're growing soft, Keleher."

"Yes? We don't elect our leaders, Starbuck. Any time you think you want the job, you can try to take it."

Starbuck balked. "I didn't mean it, that way. I was only giving my opinion."

"Don't, unless you're prepared to defend it—and yourself."

"I'm sorry." But Starbuck's eyes were smoldering.

"Get back to the encampment then. I'll expect you here with the rest of our people day after tomorrow. Can't make up your mind where you belong, can you?" Keleher pointed with amusement to the buckskin kneepads.

"I know you're trying to goad me," Starbuck whined.

"Maybe."

"You don't like me."

"As a type, Starbuck. Personally, I'm indifferent."

That was goading of a more subtle sort, but it was lost on Starbuck. Diane's indifference would irk him; Keleher's indifference was at times preferable. "We ought to be friends," Starbuck boomed. "I'm generally recognized as your second in command."

"Only because I want it that way. Amos Westler, for example has forgotten more than you will ever learn."

"That's clever," declared Starbuck. "That's expert. You play us off one against another and keep the power for yourself."

Keleher shrugged massive shoulders. "It wasn't original with me. But you're unusually perceptive today, Starbuck. And I'll say this: you've got more spunk than Westler, for all his brains."

"He's soft."

"You bring our people. I'll wait. Tell your men that since they have to pack our tents and cart our belongings, they'll be able to rest when we reach our new encampment. My group will set the place up."

"He ought to be a hermit, that Amos Westler."

Keleher shook his head. "Too scholarly. No outdoor know-how. Give him a book and he's happy. He wouldn't last a week. But he's still a good man, Starbuck. We need men like Amos Westler."

"And we need men like me."

Keleher grinned. "You should have let me say that. Trouble with you is you try to ape me. I'm always a step ahead of you, though. "And don't forget it."

"Maybe someday I'll catch up."

"That would be interesting," admitted Keleher, dismissing Starbuck with a shrug and issuing instructions as his men began to assemble their bivouac.

Starbuck sensed he had been bested in the verbal battle; but was too petulantly egotistical to admit it even to himself. Instead, he made plans for his return to the encampment. He hoped the new Shining One, that Johnny Hope kid who Diane had nursed back to health, would be foolish enough to return. Without Keleher around to steal the show, Starbuck might make himself a hero.

IF it weren't for the tawny-haired girl who had saved his life, Johnny never would have returned to the encampment of the Shining Ones. He left DeReggio with the intention of again heading north toward New York, but his way led him close by the encampment and he remembered the sudden touch of the girl's hand and before that the vision of her face, lovely and comforting, while he burned with the fever. Calling himself a fool, he entered the encampment warily, half-expecting a dozen men to leap at him with the word traitor on their lips.

But the camp was almost deserted and no one paid him any heed. He found Diane returning from the hunt with a small deer, its antlers not yet branching, slung across her shoulders. She dropped the dead animal with a happy shout and ran to Johnny.

"I'm so glad you're back."

"I'm glad to see you, too."

Then the smile left her face. "Did you—warn them?"

Johnny considered his answer. Well, he had returned because he wanted to see the girl. It would be senseless if he were not honest with her. "I had to," he said.

She nodded slowly. "It isn't hard for me to understand. They were your people. But tell me, does anyone know?"

"I'm not sure. When they find the village deserted and probably burned, though, they'll know."

"Yes," Diane agreed with him, then snapped her fingers. "But not if I say you were with me all the time. See...you even went out hunting with me. We caught this fawn together."

"You'd be lying to protect me. You may get yourself into trouble."

"How? It's my word against a lot of guessing."

"I can't let you take the chance."

"It's no chance at all. I want to do it. I want you to be one of us, Johnny. We all don't raid the villages. I don't raid them, do I?"

"No, but I—"

"But nothing. You came back here, didn't you? No one forced you."

"I came back to see you, I guess."

"Well, you're going to stay with us. A man wasn't meant to live alone like a hermit. Here..." Diane took his hand and led him forward, "...you can stay in my tent for now. It would be silly to build yourself one since we're going to move the encampment as soon as Keleher returns from the raid."

"I can't—I mean—"

"Can't, nothing. I'm a good girl, Johnny. Make no mistakes. Touch me at night and I'll scream. But I trust you...and I like you."

Her frankness was both charming and unnerving. He wanted to say he liked her too, but could not bring himself to utter the words. Instead he slipped his arm about her waist and walked with her to the tent, where she skinned the fawn expertly and prepared it for cooking. By then Johnny was sound asleep and did not wake up until Diane stirred him and offered him a platter of tender young venison.

SHORTLY after noon the next day, Starbuck returned with his men. Those who had remained behind were disappointed because the raiding party had come back empty-handed. Starbuck wasted no time adding fuel to the fire. "Has anyone seen that traitor, Johnny Hope?" he demanded.

"You mean the new man, the one Diane brought?" someone asked him. "He's here."

"The ingrate, the dirty ingrate," Starbuck boomed so all the encampment heard him. "One of us saved his life and first chance he gets he turns traitor. Next thing you know he'll want us to be conscripted by the Robots."

"You should talk," Diane cried as she and Johnny emerged from her tent. "You're always talking about how nice it would be to live with the Robots. Johnny isn't like that at all."

Starbuck raised a finger to his lips and whispered, "Keep it quiet. If they hear about this, they'll lynch Johnny."

"All of a sudden you want to keep it quiet," Diane hissed at him.

"That's right, softly."

"Well, for your information, Johnny was with me all along. We went hunting yesterday, just the two of us. Didn't we, Johnny?"

Johnny mumbled something under his breath and waited for Starbuck to speak. Suddenly the man was shouting again. He slapped Diane on the shoulder, smiled, and roared: "Thank you, Diane, thank you. I thought so. Did you all hear her? Diane told me she saw this man sneak off to warn Hamilton Village yesterday."

"That's a rotten lie!" Diane cried.

But Starbuck smiled blandly. "That's all right. I know you didn't want him to know you told me, but there's nothing to worry about. You all heard her, didn't you?"

"We heard her whispering something to you." one of the men admitted.

"She whispered because she didn't want the traitor to hear. She was afraid. She should have known we'd protect her. I'm surprised at you, Diane."

For answer, she flew at him with her knife. He laughed softly, so softly that only she heard it. A shocked look appeared on his face as he parried the blow, twisted her arm up, spun her around and held her that way while she writhed helplessly and dropped the knife to the ground. "I don't know what's the matter with you," he said. He still looked shocked.

"That should be proof enough," she panted. "I never told Starbuck what he claims."

"If you're covering up I can only assume you went with him. I am deeply shocked."

"I did not go with him. I was hunting."

"Then you admit he went!"

"I didn't admit anything. You are hurting me."

Starbuck's big hand had twisted her wrist painfully. He gave no indication of letting her go.

"She said that you're hurting her," Johnny snarled. "Let her go—"

"I'm all right," Diane said.

Starbuck was going to let her go, but Johnny did not wait. He circled Starbuck's arm with his hand and wrenched until the bigger man bellowed and released Diane.

"Good," Johnny said. "I have no fight with you, but—" He had turned to look at Diane when Starbuck's balled fist slammed against the side of his jaw, knocking him down.

HE sat there dazed, uncomprehending because he had not seen the blow coming. But Starbuck stood above him, fists clenched, and that was enough to tell him. "I still have no fight with you," Johnny said softly. He thought he could have taken the bigger man and at this moment could think of nothing he would rather do, but Starbuck had already accused Diane of being his accomplice and he did not want to involve the girl further. He hoped Starbuck would be content to boast about this one-punch victory instead.

"Scared?" Starbuck leered down at him, prodding his ribs with one foot.

"Get up and punch his teeth in," Diane pleaded.

But Johnny remained sitting on the ground, and shook his head. He explored his jaw gingerly with the fingers of one hand as if the thought of rising to take more of the same frightened him. His time of reckoning with Starbuck would come, he promised himself but now wasn't the time, not when it might involve Diane.

"You're not going to sit there?" Diane insisted. "Don't just sit there!"

Johnny shrugged. "Fighting him won't prove anything." He climbed to his feet and retreated out of Starbuck's range. He was the picture of abject cowardice and hoped it would inflate Starbuck's ego sufficiently to make him forget the charges he had brought against Diane. Starbuck was smiling smugly and booming something about letting Keleher decide what to do about Johnny after they moved the encampment. But when Johnny stalked away from him toward Diane, calling her name, she presented him only with a stiff, haughty back and by the time he reached the tent the flap was down and tied securely. Johnny heard sobbing from within.

A few moments later Starbuck and another man came and led him to a different tent where he remained under guard until the encampment had been broken, the tents and equipment packed and ready to move, the people assembled in the square clearing, which now was dotted with folded tents and bedding rolls.

"Let's move it!" Starbuck roared in his booming voice. The men stooped for their burdens, the few horses carried three and four times their normal loads. Starbuck waved the group forward dramatically, aware of his moment and making the most of it. They marched double-file into the narrow ravine and were soon well on their way toward where Keleher waited.

CHAPTER FOUR

63-17-B was twenty years old, but a trip to the repair bays every time he returned to New York City kept his beryl-steel body gleaming as if it had rolled but yesterday from the assembly lines. Now 63-17-B could sense a stiffness in the second joint of his left leg and suspected corrosion. He was looking forward with keen anticipation to the time, in the near future, when he would stretch out in the repair bay and have his worn parts exchanged.

That, however, was not on his primary level of thought. While not unique with 63-17-B, the secondary level was not universal among the robots, for the idea of individual sentience had crept into the original plans only accidentally. On his primary level of thought, 63-17-B was in closer rapport with Central Intelligence than the three hundred robots stretched out in a long, sun-reflecting line behind him. Like Central Intelligence itself, and unlike the few humans who thought of such things, 63-17-B believed that matter and energy are not merely components of one another but are actually the same thing. Thus he explained his greater primary level of thought by saying that the energy-matter bridge connecting him with Central Intelligence, invisible but measurable in quanta as was his body, was stronger than most. On the social level, this gave 63-17-B leadership of the three hundred.

Thought-quanta crackled back and forth between 63-17-B and Central Intelligence in New York and, as on all such occasions, 63-17-B was not sure how much of the conversation reached the other Robots. "Hamilton Village is aflame," 63-17-B thought.

"Did you fire it?" The answer was immediate—and angry.

"Certainly not. We arrived too late to prevent it."

"Yet your scouts reported the Village was going to move out. You know a moving Village may or may not remain together. As often as not, it separates into small bands, which will spread out and find their way to distant communities. An ideal means of spreading the Plague, although I need not remind you of that."

"I am aware—"

"The error is unpardonable, unless the Villagers have not yet fled."

"Unfortunately, they have."

"Then another opportunity slips through our fingers. 63-17-B, upon your return you are to report to the Intelligence bays for a reexamination of your rapport synapses."

"But—"

"But nothing." The thought-communication crackled to silence.

63-17-B made the mental equivalent of a sigh. Such re-examinations, he knew from bitter experience, were shams. Re-shuffling was more like it. At a whim of Central Intelligence he might become nothing but a second-class Robot. On the surface, Intelligence would discover a flaw in his synapses. Actually, Intelligence would produce the flaw and pass his mantle of leadership down the line to some other Robot.

Sullenly, 63-17-B called a halt. Like all Robots, he was vindictive. Constructed originally as machines of war, the Robots had had revenge built into their mind-patterns as a strong factor. Actually, second-class Robots were not aware of this. The feelings merely existed and they acted accordingly. But 63-17-B was only too acutely aware. It pained him. The Robots had never actually functioned as machines of war, for the War had taken a bacteriological turn before the mechanical infantry could march off to battle.

The Robots had been stored as useless while disease swept Earth—with the development of the Plague itself making all further fighting impossible on an international scale. But the

Plague got out of hand, 63-17-B remembered dimly. The slightest contact meant almost certain contamination and mankind prepared grimly for the end of its brief dominion over the Earth—until someone thought of the Robots. Let them cure the Plague; the antidote was known, they merely had to apply it. 63-17-B's memory coils tightened angrily. Until that time, the Robots had been slighted, although they had waited patiently to serve their masters. Masters, indeed. 63-17-B recognized the vindictive pattern of his thoughts for what it was: mankind had had its chance and had failed. After man—the Robots. It was as simple as that.

But now 63-17-B was seething. He'd been advancing steadily in the Robot-hierarchy and had even expected himself to be assigned to Central Intelligence itself before too long. Because the impetuous people of Hamilton Village had set their city to the torch before he could arrive, all was lost.

He scanned the surrounding countryside with photo-retinal cells. Far below, just leaving the edge of the burning town, were a pair of stragglers—man and woman, he thought, but couldn't be sure at this distance. Well, revenge on two individuals would be better than nothing...

Strong hauling ropes were prepared, and now 63-17-B could see the figures were not two, but three. Since his photo-retinal cells could not perceive color except as shades of black and white, he had no way of telling the three figures were not Villagers but Shining Ones.

"WE'RE approaching Hamilton Village," said Starbuck over his shoulder as Diane overtook him at the head of the column to get her first look at the place. "You can see the flames."

"I thought you said the fire was almost out when you left Keleher and the others."

"I did, but you can't predict those things. Apparently it has started again. See?"

They had reached a rise of ground and could see what was left of the village in a broad valley below them, a great pall of black smoke rising from it sluggishly. Starbuck saw something else a few miles off to the north, but said nothing. It was a long, thin column, gleaming metallically. At this distance he could not be sure, but it looked like a line of Robots.

"Keleher and the others are close by," Starbuck said mechanically. He was not thinking of Keleher. The trouble with this group of Shining Ones was that no one understood Starbuck. Not only were his talents for leadership unappreciated, he was actually made fun of. He'd been sullen ever since his mental rebuff at the hands of Keleher. He'd acted inconsistently. His anger had been a free-floating thing, and he'd very nearly got Diane in trouble for it.

That was ridiculous. The answer seemed obvious enough: if one is not appreciated in a particular place, one should go elsewhere. There was Thomas Burwood, a youngster whose father had been chief before Keleher and who had been killed *by* Keleher. Burwood almost certainly would join Starbuck. And Diane could be taken by force if necessary.

Starbuck put the stocky man named Gilbert in charge of the column and sought out Burwood. He found the younger man on a fringe of the column, plodding listlessly along.

"Listen, Tom," said Starbuck in a confidential voice. "We've often talked about life among the Robots, but we're letting our years fritter away. What would you do if the opportunity presented itself?"

Like Starbuck himself, Burwood was an over-sized young man given to fits of temperament. "What's the use?" he said. "You can't just walk into the Robot Citadel. They would kill you first and ask questions afterwards."

"No, but you could join Robots in the field. It's done that way most of the time, since the Robots venture forth either to spread the Plague or gain conscripts among the Shining Ones." Starbuck whispered in his best confidential voice, "And, Tom, there's a group of Robots two or three miles from here right now. What do you say to that?"

"Let me think." Burwood frowned. "I don't know. It's one

thing to talk about it but another to—"

"Keleher didn't give your father a chance to think, did he? Not when your father was growing old and Keleher knew he could take him. He killed him, struck him down like an animal, don't forget that, Tom."

"That's true, but—"

"You're worrying about life among the Robots, are you? From every rumor I've heard, you can live like a king, like the days before World War III ruined our civilization. What do you say, Tom? An opportunity like this doesn't often come."

"Well—"

"Of course, if you're afraid…but I thought you were made of the same stuff as your father, the only leader I have ever served faithfully."

"That's enough, Harry!" Young Burwood's voice broke. "I'll go with you."

"I knew you would. You're just like your father, Tom. There's one thing I want to do first…" The two whispered together for a time, then Starbuck drifted back toward the rear of the column and permitted himself to straggle until he was out of sight of the rear guard, first making arrangements for the prisoner, Johnny Hope, to be taken off the trail into the woods. Tom Burwood, meanwhile, double-timed up toward the head of the column.

"DIANE, I was looking for you."

"Hello, Tom. What is it?"

"Some one wants to see you. Rear of the column."

"Who?" All through their march, Diane had wanted to make her peace with Johnny, but the opportunity had never presented itself.

"I'm not at liberty to say," Burwood told her slyly, and winked.

"Is it Johnny?"

Burwood smiled affably. "I can't say. Please, Diane. I was only told to fetch you. It's been arranged temporarily, but he can't remain back there indefinitely."

"I'm coming. Lead the way," Diane said eagerly, and fell into step with Burwood. Johnny must have had his reasons for not fighting with Starbuck. He was not the cowardly type, unless Diane had suddenly become a bad judge of people. Perhaps he thought, in some strange way, he was protecting her...

"Where is he, Tom? I don't see anyone."

"A little further."

"But we've already left the column."

"Just around that clump of trees, I think."

Something rustled in the undergrowth. "Johnny?" Diane called expectantly.

He stepped out into the trail and faced her. It was Harry Starbuck.

"What kind of a joke is this?" Diane demanded angrily, turning to rejoin the column. "I thought I was coming back here to meet Johnny."

Burwood laughed easily. "I never said that."

"Well, whatever you're planning you can count me out. Of all the nerve, bringing me back here like this—"

"Would you like to see Johnny alive?" Starbuck asked in a conversational tone.

"What do you mean by that?"

"That you had better cooperate with me, Diane. The three of us are leaving the column now, you, Tom and I. If you don't, I can't guarantee anything about Johnny."

Diane did not know whether to believe him or not, but she would hardly endanger Johnny's life on a notion.

"I'll go with you," she said.

Less than an hour later, they approached the vanguard of the file of Robots. Burwood and Diane saw them at the same time, contempt filling Diane's eyes as she began to understand what had been on Starbuck's mind. Fear was there too, threatening to unnerve her at any moment, but the scorn she felt for Starbuck prevented it from overpowering her. "Of all the cheap tricks," she said. "You—you wanted to join the Robots, but you also wanted me. Johnny was never in any danger. It was all a lie, to get me here. Well, if you think I'm going with you—" Diane crouched abruptly, came up with a handful of dry earth and flung it at Starbuck's face, blinding him. Then she began to run.

"Get her, Burwood!" Starbuck roared. "Don't let her escape."

It wasn't Burwood's fight, but if he had thrown in with Starbuck he wanted to remain in the man's good graces, at least until he could figure things out for himself. Besides, his first sight of the Robots had almost choked him with fear. Chasing Diane would take his mind off them. He set out after her, aware that a still half-blinded Starbuck was circling around in another direction.

Diane guessed her best chance for escape would lie along the very edge of the file of Robots. She did not relish the idea, but she had seen the look on Burwood's face when the creatures of metal had appeared and figured he would be loathe to follow her in that direction.

Did the Robots see her? She ran in their direction, her clothing catching and tearing on the undergrowth. She neared the head of the file and could hear Burwood stumbling along behind her. The metal figures stood there, unmoving— watching her? Each one twelve feet tall, they could have stamped her to death.

BEHIND her, Diane heard a hoarse scream. She whirled instinctively, lost her footing, fell. One of the Robots had taken Burwood, who was thrashing and kicking helplessly as it bore him aloft and held him feet pounding on air, two yards off the ground.

She didn't like Burwood, but she had nothing against him. He screamed again, his voice breaking.

"Put him down," Diane shouted. She might as well have been talking to the ingots from which the Robots had been fashioned for all the heed they paid her. She whirled again, sought Starbuck, but couldn't find him. Starbuck always talked of the Robots, perhaps he knew how to communicate with them.

Now the Robot had set a trembling Burwood down on the ground. Now a great noose of rope was drawn about his neck, its other end slung over the branch of a huge, bare-limbed tree. Now...

Something neither warm nor cold touched Diane, grasped her about the middle and lifted her. It was a nightmare. It was unreal, not happening to her. The ground spun giddily, all vision receded behind a wave of vertigo, then returned, still spinning.

Diane clawed at the metal head, at the hard, unblinking eyes, scraping uselessly. She might as well try to scrape down the side of a mountain with her fingernails.

Burwood was hanging.

Feet dangling, arms bound behind him, he twisted and writhed in his last death agony. Diane shuddered, turning away, striking her head sharply against the hard metal of the Robot. When her vision cleared again, she was on the ground, another Robot stalking soundlessly toward her for all its great bulk, a noose identical to the one from which Burwood dangled suspended from its metal hand.

But the scene had changed, Diane realized wildly. A great airship, a rocket, had landed midway between the file of Robots and the burning village. Vaguely, she remembered that Starbuck had once said only Robots from the Citadel itself used the rockets, since only a few remained from man's last great War.

Starbuck was nearby, shaking but holding his ground, shouting at the Robots as if his very life depended on it. And, Diane thought despairingly, it did.

"Leave her be!" Starbuck cried. "You're making a terrible mistake. We're not from the village. We're Shining Ones. We're Shining Ones, I tell you. We came here to join you, to be conscripted. We want to work for the Robots. See, we're Shining Ones!"

Did they understand? Diane couldn't tell. The Robots with the noose reached down and grabbed her, drawing her aloft again. She wanted to scream, but all her energy could bring forth only a whimper. She wanted to shut her eyes tightly and wake up, trembling but otherwise all right, in her tent. She could feel a lurching motion as the Robot began to move.

Burwood hung slackly now, twisting gently from side to side, like a rag doll, with the motion of the rope. Diane fainted.

Within half an hour, all the Robots had filed into their waiting ship. It blasted skyward on a jet of flame that was all but lost against the fires that consumed Hamilton Village.

CHAPTER FIVE

"WILL Harry Starbuck please step forth and make his report?" One of Keleher's assistants brought the command to the Shining Ones who had joined the larger group near Hamilton Village.

There was a silence.

"Where is Starbuck?"

No one knew. The assistant shook his head and returned to Keleher for further instructions. Had anyone seen Starbuck? A short while ago, yes. Not for the past hour, though. Keleher next called for Diane, who had found Johnny Hope, the alleged traitor, along with Starbuck.

Some of them had seen her marching toward the rear of the column with Tom Burwood not long since. She did not answer the summons. And Burwood could not be found anywhere.

"Is everyone going crazy?" Keleher stormed. "Fetch the prisoner himself. We'll see what's going on."

Moments later: "Hope, charges have been brought against you concerning our raid on Hamilton Village."

"I know all about the charges. I refuse to discuss them now."

Keleher smiled without mirth. "You—refuse?"

"They were looking for Diane. They couldn't find her. They

were looking for Starbuck too, and couldn't find him. It's Starbuck who's made the accusation, so we'll have to wait until he's found. I don't care one way or the other about Starbuck, but I want to find Diane."

Plump Gilbert came forward said, "I may be able to shed some light on this. After Starbuck gave me charge of the column he conferred with Tom Burwood for a time, then disappeared. But Burwood whispered something to Diane and she joined him, heading for the rear of the column."

"You see?" Johnny demanded. "Starbuck went someplace with Diane. From the looks of it, she was tricked into going with him."

"Mere supposition," said Keleher, "although I wouldn't trust Starbuck particularly."

"Listen," Johnny went on, "that girl saved my life. I want to find her. Since you can't try my case until Starbuck is found, let me look for them and—"

"How do we know you will return?"

"My word," said Johnny, but the look on Keleher's face said that would never satisfy him.

"If the lad promises and if meanwhile he cannot be tried…" began Gilbert.

"When I, want your advice, I'll ask for it," Keleher said curtly. "The boy stays here."

"But he merely wants to find Diane," persisted Gilbert.

"Enough. If someone thinks to depose me, let him try. Meanwhile, I command here. The boy stays. He will be considered innocent until we can bring him to trial, but he will not be permitted to leave the encampment."

"Her life may be in danger," Johnny said grimly.

"I doubt it. I have given my orders."

"They don't satisfy me," Johnny told Keleher bluntly. "Am I to be regarded as prisoner or member of the community until my trial?"

"You are one of us, a Shining One, until proven guilty. It is the way of our law."

"In that case," Johnny informed him, "I challenge your right to rule. *I* would depose you." Even as he spoke the words, Johnny doubted their wisdom. Keleher was large and powerful; Johnny had recently recovered from the Plague and did not feel fully himself. Still, he had to find Diane, and if there was no other way...

Keleher was grinning. "Perhaps you do not know what that entails. I'll admit, it's primitive. Upon your challenge we fight. Not with weapons, Johnny, but with our bare hands. Call it a peculiarity of mine, but I prefer brute strength. It is as if civilization, in closing its book for mankind, has put men like me in its stead. The ballot, the tribunal, the town meeting—all these are sophistications leading ultimately back along the road to civilization. If that means another war and a worse one, I want no part of it. Small communities, living by mean strength, fighting for their existence tooth and nail, can't start a civilization growing.

"The level I want to maintain is physical, brutal, elemental. Knowing that, do you still challenge my right?" Keleher folded huge-muscled arms across his massive chest and stared with scorn at Johnny. "Well?"

"I was aware of that. The answer is yes."

"Then we can start making arrangements for the time and place. Would you prefer it on our journey before we reach a new permanent encampment, or after we have arrived to set up camp? You still look pale from your time with the Plague, my young friend."

"I prefer it right here," Johnny said. "I can't wait. Right here, and right now."

The sudden complete silence was broken by Keleher's explosive laughter as he unbuckled his weapon-belt and let it fall with knife and club to the ground.

"WHAT do you think, Diane?"

"Don't speak to me. I think it was a dirty trick, but I should have expected it from you. And you let Tom Burwood die, too."

I couldn't do anything about that," Starbuck protested. "I tried. By the time I got through to them Burwood was already dead. As it is, I saved your life."

"For this?" Diane gestured around her scornfully, to take in the tiny cubicle aboard the rocket that they occupied. After depositing them within it ten minutes before, the Robots had ignored them.

"I'm surprised at you. Have, some patience, Diane. Someday Diane. Someday you'll be grateful I took you along. You're young, you have no idea what life could be like in a civilized place."

"Do you? How do you know how the Robots treat people?"

"I have heard rumors. We all have. But I'm older than I look. I was a small boy before the war, Diane. But I remember, I remember. The luxuries, the comforts. You'll see."

"I ought to kill you," Diane said coldly. Starbuck blanched. "I might, too, first chance I get. You're so self-centered, you're almost inhuman. But perhaps I'm stupid enough to think you'll realize your mistake someday, and two of us will have a better chance of getting away than one. I don't know. I ought to kill you, though."

"I did it for you. I wanted you with me. I couldn't enjoy the life I'm going to lead without you by my side."

"You're a fool, Harry. I can't even hate you. I feel sorry for you. What do the Robots do from day to day? You don't even know that. You haven't the slightest idea what you've let us in for. You don't even know for sure where we're going."

Starbuck shook his head. "You're wrong about that. We're going to the Citadel in New York. We should be arriving in a few minutes. You'll change your mind, Diane. Wait until you see the Citadel. Wait until—"

"You've never seen it. You're just guessing."

"It's more than a guess. It's every rumor I have ever heard. Diane, I want you to share it with me, to learn to love it with me. You're beautiful. You weren't meant for buckskins,"

Starbuck fingered the tattered clothing barely covering her torso.

"Keep away from me."

"Don't you realize it's just the two of us now—and the Robots?"

"I'm warning you."

Starbuck shrugged and sat down at the other side of the small cubicle. "You're frightened now," he said. "I've got patience, even if you haven't. Wait and see how the Robots will provide for us."

Diane shuddered and tried to hide it. Trapped aboard a ship full of Robots, she was companion to a madman. Strangely, no thought could comfort her but the image of Johnny Hope, somewhere many miles behind them, a prisoner of Keleher and the band of Shining Ones. Perhaps, she thought grimly, the madman had for company a madwoman...

THE Shining Ones were gathering not two miles above the gutted ruins of Hamilton Village. Wood had been stacked for the cook-fires, but as yet no spark had been coaxed into flame. Half the tents had been raised tautly about their ridgepoles; others were still to be unpacked. Five hundred strong, the whole group gathered around a natural clearing in the woods, where deft-fingered girls were applying grease to Keleher and Johnny.

They had stripped to their shorts, Keleher with his thick-thewed limbs glistening in the fading sunlight, arms folded like some immobile, heroic statue, all muscle and sinew, carved from granite, Johnny fidgeting, waiting for the fight to start. He was surprised at his own objective lack of fear; he wanted only to start out after Diane.

"You probably wonder why they grease you," Amos Westler declared. Westler was a small, slim man with close-cropped graying hair and eyes that would twinkle, Johnny thought, even in darkness. He had come to Johnny's corner as a sort of unexpected second, to ready him for battle. "It's a concession on the part of Keleher, Johnny. He has declared openly your strength is no match for his. The slicking will make speed and dexterity count for more."

"Am I supposed to be grateful? The only reason I'm fighting him is because he won't let me seek Diane any other way. She could be in danger right now; her life might be at stake. Keleher is a fool."

"And life among the Shining Ones has always been an expendable item. Diane's life, your life, even Keleher's."

"What happens if I win?"

Westler sighed wistfully. "You won't. This won't be the first fight for Keleher, nor the last. Actually, I hope you do win."

"Why? And you haven't answered my question."

"Because I've always wanted to leave the encampment. But I'm not a man for the outdoors, Johnny. I wouldn't survive a week. With your companionship, I might. Should you win the fight, and should you decide to seek Diane, I would like to join you."

Johnny grasped his hand, shook it. "Done," he said.

Westler smiled, wiping grease on his trousers. "To answer your question, if you win you're the chief of this encampment."

Now Johnny was smiling. "A job I'm not particularly interested in. I only want to—"

"I know. Look for the girl. During the excitement, something went entirely unnoticed. A rocket ship took off, near the ruins of the Village. Rockets mean Robots—and from the Citadel. Tell me, Johnny, if the trail leads there, will you follow?"

Johnny shrugged. "I hadn't thought of that, I didn't realize the Robots were so near."

"Then you're going to back down?" Disappointment was in Westler's expressive eyes.

"Never. I saw New York once. I stood on the Jersey cliffs at sunset and gazed across the broad river at the Citadel with its winking lights and beacons. It is not a place of fear, but a place that men built, long ago. I will certainly go."

Again Amos Westler sighed. "I hope you win this fight,

Johnny. I never wished for anything so much in my life. I was a college professor before the war and I learned this: the search for knowledge is a strange thing and knows no fear. But I am no young man, and this may be my last opportunity."

"Ready?" Keleher's voice roared across the clearing. "If the girls are finished caressing you with their oils...?"

THE girls stepped back, looked at Johnny, tall and lithe but so small compared to Keleher, and shook their heads.

"Ready," Johnny said, moving out toward Keleher warily.

"His legs," Amos Westler confided. "He uses them like another pair of arms. Watch them."

The grease on his face had been applied too close to his eyes and Johnny found he had to blink to clear his vision. Keleher came lumbering across the clearing, gathering momentum. By the time he neared Johnny he was fairly rocketing down upon him. The muttering of the assembled encampment had been stilled as if by some unspoken command. There was the sound of Keleher's thundering feet and nothing else.

The juggernaut thundered close and was almost upon him, his great arms outstretched, a huge body shining red in the last light of the sun. At the last moment, Johnny sidestepped, thrust out his leg, added momentum to Keleher with his arms as he pounded by. Something struck his leg; there was a loud, bull-bellowing cry. Keleher flipped completely over and sprawled in the dust a dozen feet away.

He came up roaring his rage as Johnny waited, balancing on the balls of his feet, fists up and ready. Keleher parried Johnny's left hand when the blow was too long in coming, struck with his own great right fist. Johnny went over on his back and felt Keleher at his throat almost before he had hit the ground. Now the crowd was churning with excitement and Johnny found himself thinking they must have smelled blood in the air.

Their heavily greased bodies prevented Keleher from applying a stranglehold. Johnny squirmed out from under, straddled the bigger man's back and felt himself borne aloft, still clinging there, as Keleher climbed to his feet and charged about the clearing. Johnny held grimly, his forearm circling the thick throat, choking off Keleher's breath. But the shaggy head twisted and broke free. The legs drummed backwards and Johnny whirled in time to fathom Keleher's plan.

He was going to crush Johnny against the bole of an oak tree, cracking his ribs and ending the battle at once. Without mirth, Johnny smiled. So intent was Keleher upon his plan, he did not bother to hold Johnny on his back. Possibly he thought that was Johnny's intention, anyway. Johnny leaped away, rolling clear, as Keleher backed into the tree trunk with all the strength of his huge muscles.

There was a terrible crunching sound as Keleher hit the tree and went down as if axed. Groggily, he began to rise, but Johnny was waiting for him, waiting to see if there was any fight left in the half-conscious man. The eyes were watery, the lips slack, the arms twitching. Johnny waited...

"Stop!" someone cried. "I bring news."

At first the encampment shouted him down, but presently Johnny became aware of loud talking, of angry shouts, of a buzzing, as from a sundered hornets' nest, which swept the clearing. He whirled to face the newcomer as Keleher slumped at his feet, clawing the ground and gasping, "I don't...surrender...Johnny. Only give...me...time to catch my wind...and..."

THEY turned to Johnny, all of them, their new leader. For Keleher had spoken those words, then fell forward on his face. Three men carried him off to a tent, where two women brought vessels of water.

"They went looking for the three missing ones, Hope."

"What can we do?"

"The Robots."

"Tell us, Hope."

"What they did once, they might do again."

Johnny laughed as reaction from his ordeal set in. They

crowded around him, flies swarming for honey. They hadn't given him a chance in the fight, but now because Keleher had cracked his own ribs instead of Johnny's, Johnny was their leader. It was a job he neither wanted nor would tolerate.

"What they're trying to say," Amos Westler told him, "is that they found Tom Burwood not far from here."

"What about Diane?" Johnny demanded eagerly.

"No Diane, no Starbuck. They found Burwood, hanging by his neck, dead."

"Dead?" Johnny said, dazed. "Diane?"

"You're not listening to me, young man. Diane they were not able to find." Then, as if Westler suddenly realized he was addressing the encampment's new—though admittedly bewildered—leader, he apologized. "I'm sorry. While Burwood's corpse was the only one they found, there were shreds of clothing in the undergrowth. There—"

"Diane?" Johnny cut in.

"Possibly...they're not sure. I would say all indications point to the Robot Citadel. You said you would go, but now that you are our leader, perhaps you've changed your mind. When leadership is thrust upon a man—"

"When an old leader is vanquished," plump Gilbert bubbled effusively, "there is a celebration, sir. And there is an edict to be handed down by the new leader. Do we banish Keleher from the encampment when his condition permits? Do we slay him for you? Do we—"

"Do whatever you want," Johnny said irritably. "I'm not staying."

"This is some kind of a joke!" Gilbert exclaimed.

"I have nothing against Keleher," Johnny replied. "And I still have nothing against him. I'm simply leaving. When Keleher regains consciousness, when his body heals, you may tell him for me that I choose not to depose him. He is still your leader."

"That is clearly impossible," Gilbert stated matter-of-factly.

"Is it? I command you in this. Keleher remains on as chief.

But tell him this for me: some day I may call upon him and his people for help, and when I do…"

"You have vision," said Amos Westler, admiration in his voice.

"When I do, I want no delays. That is my message to your ruler…to Keleher. Is it understood?"

Gilbert and some of the others nodded. A small, intense man, Westler fidgeted about impatiently while the girls returned with thick strips of cloth and scrubbed the grease from Johnny.

"I'm now a celebrity," he said to Westler, feeling himself briefly as one with these wild people as they gathered around for his advice, preparing a victory banquet over roaring fires as darkness covered the bivouac area. He munched a savory leg of fowl, slaked his thirst from a moist leather wine bag, the claret stream gushing into his mouth from the spout.

"You see," Westler could not hide his disappointment. "It is even as I said. You will stay."

Johnny grinned at him. "Are you tired?"

"Why, no."

Tossing a chicken bone into the fire, Johnny went on: "And do you know the way to New York in the darkness?"

"No—o."

"I think I do. Are you ready to start?"

"Are you serious?" Westler cried. "Do you mean that, Johnny?"

"Let's go." And not waiting for an answer, Johnny clapped Gilbert on the back, told him to take charge until Keleher had recovered, and left the clearing with Westler trailing at his heels.

The night closed in about them, not quiet, but alive with the sounds of insects and the occasional soft-pad-padding of small hunting animals. Johnny set a quick, mile-eating pace that made Westler's breath wheeze in and out of his lungs asthmatically, but the older man did not complain once.

CHAPTER SIX

"WE have openings in the repair bays or for servants among the inner circle of Shining Ones who work hand in hand with our masters," the old woman told Starbuck and Diane after they had been taken from the rocket ship in New York and shunted underground where the subways had been converted into living quarters for humans without being given a chance to see the city. "Which will it be?"

"We're not cut out to be menials," Starbuck said coldly, "but the repair bays don't appeal to me, either. You say servants to the leaders themselves?"

"To the top echelon of Shining Ones who serve the metal masters, yes. You will find the socioeconomic hierarchy rigidly enforced here. Well, which will it be?"

Starbuck had heard about palace revolutions. It would be servants to the leaders, naturally. Let them bide their time, let them learn what they could of the Citadel and its Robots. "Servants," he said.

"Are you married?" The old woman, shamelessly bare to the waist on this hot day, smiled at them with a perfect set of false teeth which seemed laughably incongruous in her gaunt, seamed face. Her bare breasts were dry as parchment and hung, flat but pendulant, almost to her waist. From a distance she looked almost like a manikin, a leathery, humanoid robot.

"We are," Starbuck beamed.

But Diane said, "Certainly not."

The old woman cackled. "I believe the woman. In that case, you will live in these underground dormitories."

"Not in the City upstairs?" Starbuck demanded, disappointed.

"Not in the City, that is correct. Do not ask why, it is merely so. We work for the Robots and obey them, is that clear? Some day the only humans left on Earth will be Shining Ones, or so the Robots tell us. Then we will climb up into the light of day and take our rightful place, side by side with them. Meanwhile, we do as we are told."

"Are you satisfied, Harry?" Diane wanted to know. "The Robots make promises—and destroy our brothers."

"Our brothers?" Starbuck laughed. "You mean the people of the villages? Those…our brothers?"

"The Plague makes brother hate brother, but you're a fool, Starbuck. The Robots want that, this playing of human against human."

"Yes? How do you know? You've never…"

"I don't know. But Amos Westler always said so."

"Westler!" Starbuck spat contemptuously. "A reader of books. We go out to hunt or raid, Westler seeks his books and grows soft looking through them."

"With more Westlers and less Starbucks in the world," Diane began, "we probably wouldn't have had to fight three World Wars and never would have—"

"That's enough," said Starbuck, his eyes darting suspiciously to the old woman, who was taking in their conversation with an amused look on her face.

"It is quite enough," agreed the old woman. "If you want to last here more than a few days."

"Can the Robots actually understand us?" Starbuck asked.

The old woman shrugged thin shoulders. "Some say they can read our minds. It is not important. Those of us who rule can understand. Since they can somehow communicate with the Robots, it is the same thing."

"We will conform," promised Starbuck.

"Like robots of robots," said Diane bitterly.

JOHNNY Hope rubbed the stubble of beard on his face and frowned at Westler. "I'm not sure, but I think I know this place. We should reach the New York River this afternoon."

They stood in a forest glade not a hundred yards from one of the overgrown concrete highways upon which the Robots were known to tread. A path paralleled the highway through the woods, and upon this they made their way.

"Sometimes I wonder if you know what you're letting yourself in for," Westler mused.

"I want to find Diane. I'll take whatever goes with it."

"Do you mind if I ask why?"

"I'm not sure I know myself. All I know is I think of her all the time. Nothing matters as much as finding her—and freeing her."

"We could be wrong. Perhaps she is not with the Robots at all."

"What do you think?" Hope responded. "Do you think she is or do you think she isn't?"

"I think she is. Everything points to it. I was only pointing out that we're not sure. Listen, Johnny, not many years ago I met a man, another Shining One, who had fled from New York. He was old and dying so he didn't last long, but he told me about things that—"

"About the Robots, you mean?"

"Yes. You probably know, of course, that they can help cure the Plague. But instead, they spread it."

"I never could figure out why."

"Who knows what sort of thinking the Robots can do? We're not even sure if they possess sentience at all, although I suspect they do. But in the last days of the War, man made a frantic mistake. The Robots were conceived as fighters, were constructed as fighters, were built to hate man and to kill man. When we gave the Robots a different mission entirely, it failed. They've simply strengthened the Plague toxoid and made it lethal. I don't think they'll rest until every man on Earth is destroyed.

"We're weak now, disorganized. We've left civilization behind us. You'd think the Robots could do the job overnight, but the only thing that prevents them, actually, is their lack of numbers."

"Most of my people—I mean the villagers, not my people any longer—most of them believe the Robots somehow *will* cure the Plague," Hope stated matter-of-factly.

"And most of my people," responded Westler, "believe their destiny is hand in glove with the destiny of the Robots. They put it this way: we are hated by the rest of mankind, we are apparently not hated by the Robots. Why not cooperate with them then? Actually, a free band of Shining Ones as large as Keleher's is the exception, not the rule. Every day, more and more Shining Ones go to the Citadel in New York or elsewhere to work for the Robots. Not a pretty picture, is it?"

"What can we do about it?"

"At present, I don't have the slightest notion. We've got to do something, though. Someone's got to do something, unless nature's ready to write off mankind as a bad experiment. Perhaps I am a pedant, Johnny. I do not know. But I will tell you this: when all the great strides in human history were made, it was the pedants, the scholars who paved the way. I want to see the Citadel not only to learn, but to see if there is something, some way, to end the reign of the Robots. It seems incredible that men, their makers, lacked the foresight to equip them with an Achilles Heel, if the need ever arose."

ABRUPTLY, Johnny motioned Westler down with a wave of his hand. "It looks like you're going to find out soon enough. Take a look."

Johnny parted the bushes in front of them. Here the dirt path had angled sharply toward the highway so that not more than thirty yards separated them. Marching silently along the concrete in the direction of New York, quiet but for the clanking of their joints, was a long file of Robots.

"Spongy metal foot-pads," whispered Westler, staring eagerly at the Robots. "We built fine fighting machines, Johnny, and now we find that we have to suffer the consequences."

Johnny nodded impatiently, hardly feeling philosophical. "This is what we came here for, Amos," he said. "Afraid?"

"To tell you the truth, I'm not sure yet."

Johnny was not sure, either, but he did not want to brood about it. He stood up recklessly, forcing his way through the undergrowth toward the highway. By the time he reached it, Westler trailing uncertainly at his heels, he was shouting. It worked magically. The long line of Robots, extending as far as they could see to the left and several hundred yards to the right, stopped its steady advance. The great metal heads, each bigger than a man, swiveled on the sockets that joined them with the tiny bodies. The unblinking eyes that now faced them—another set for each Robot surveyed the rear, Johnny knew—were lined up row on row.

"We want to join you," Johnny called out. "We want employment in the Citadel." Did a human ask a Robot for employment? Johnny hardly knew, for nothing had been further from his mind until recently.

The leading Robot came back down the line toward them. Johnny could read nothing in the artificial eyes and had to check a wild impulse to run.

"Sometimes I prefer the uncomplicated life of an unimaginative man of action," Westler moaned softly.

It was, Johnny knew, a good point He did not bother telling Westler that both traits had merged in him, which might have been better or worse, depending upon the circumstances.

Then the Robot was upon them.

CHAPTER SEVEN

"63-17-B?"

"Yes, sir?" All Robots, even those with a primary level of thought as high as 63-17-B and an existing secondary level, addressed Central Intelligence as sir.

"After exhaustive tests, it has been adjudged that an over-estimation has been made regarding your mental ability. Since that is the case, it will mechanically be necessary to change your position."

Sullenly, plotting shapeless revenge at a Central Intelligence that would never consider the possibility of an outside factor intervening unexpectedly and hence altering or spoiling what had been planned, 63-17-B listened to his fate.

"A position currently is vacant as supervisor of the Shining Ones in a section of the repair bays. Do you have any objections to assuming this new duty in place of the old?"

To object was disastrous. To object was to admit you needed not merely a lesser job commensurate with your lesser skill but also complete readjustment of your thinking process. "No objections at all, sir," thought 63-17-B, all the while smoldering with resentment. His time would come. What was the old human expression about every dog having his day?

"Then you will report at once to repair bay 151. Do you know its location?"

"I will find it." That was the prescribed answer. One rarely asked questions. One found out for oneself from Central Information. 63-17-B half thought he was still being tested in some less-obvious and hence all the more deadly fashion. But to be placed in charge of a gang of humans! It was degrading.

"In time, 63-17-B, you shall be tested again. If it is our opinion you have gained back what we thought you once possessed, you will again be elevated to a higher station."

63-17-B cursed Central Intelligence on a private wavelength. Central Intelligence was the creator of perfect plans. If a plan misfired, Central Intelligence could not be held responsible. Since accidents of nature had never been considered valid excuses, blame always fell on the executing Robot. Until recently, 63-17-B had managed to beat the system, largely through luck. Now while he realized it was the most mechanical thing in the world to do as you were told, he could not hide his bitter disappointment. But he pushed it from his mind all at once when he felt another mind nibbling at his private wavelength. No one could be trusted, not when each Robot tried to outdo every other Robot in the eyes of Central Intelligence, not when private thoughts could be intercepted by monitors, not when communal thinking was considered preferable to individual thinking. That thought made 63-17-B shudder, his joints clanking as a sudden surge of power, the electrical equivalent of adrenal secretions, coursed through his frame. He was indeed thinking not along the prescribed lines. Probably something was wrong with him.

"THIS is ironical," said Amos Westler as the first inert Robot came sliding down the conveyor belt where it stopped—a rusted man-shaped creature twice man's size with huge conical head and withdrawn antenna—in front of his bench. "We'll never learn anything this way. You won't learn the whereabouts of Diane at this bench, and I won't learn what I've come to find out."

"We're not on duty twenty-four hours a day," Johnny reminded him, unfastening leg-joints with a large, wrench-like instrument and wiping the parts with an oily rag before he reassembled them. "If Diane is here, I'll find her."

"Well, we've learned nothing so far. They took us into the Citadel through a tile-walled tunnel—"

"Surely one of the wonders of the world!" Johnny cried, remembering.

"The world has many wonders, natural and man-made, if we could but see them. Anyway, they then deposited us in those underground quarters where all the humans seem to live here. The old hag interviewed us—"

"Yes. She wouldn't say if she'd seen Starbuck and Diane or not when I described them, but it sure made her smile. I think they're here in the Citadel, Amos."

"—then assigned us to this repair bay for work. Do you realize that except for the brief time it took to go from the tunnel exit to the underground quarters, we haven't seen the light of day. Try learning something in these, these caves!"

Without warning, the conveyor belts were stilled. Hidden lighting in the walls flared brighter as a group of Robots entered the large vault.

"ATTENTION!" A voice blared at them, oddly metallic. Johnny could not tell where it came from. "Robot 63-17-B is now entering the vault. As your supervisor, 63-17-B is to be obeyed as if he were Central Intelligence itself. He is to be addressed not directly, but through your human supervisor."

The Robot numbered 63-17-B (but the numbers were hidden under the central face plate and you hardly could tell the machines apart) made a brief inspection of the vault, then climbed to his niche in the wall, where he sat completely without motion while the other Robots filed from the chamber.

"Although we can't address the Robot, our supervisor can," Westler said eagerly. "That means, at least, communication of some sort is possible."

"I guess so. Why don't you get to know the supervisor?"

"You're much better at that sort of thing than I am, Johnny."

"We came here for different reasons, don't forget. There's an old hag I'd like to answer more questions when I find her."

"Here comes our supervisor now," Westler whispered. Then, aloud: "My name is Amos Westler."

"I don't care what it is. It's recorded. Keep working, friend." The supervisor was a brutal-faced man who snarled out his words. His jaw, cheekbones and forehead were silver-sheened with Plague scar, with the Plague silver remaining there as well as on his limbs. His face seemed metallic as a Robot's.

"See?" Westler whispered in despair as another damaged Robot slid to a stop in front of them.

Johnny offered a wan grin. "Take it easy," he said, but he hardly felt more than the last remaining shreds of patience within himself. If the old hag wouldn't talk when he saw her tonight...

"DON'T bother calling me names, young man," cackled the hag. "I'm virtually immune. It is against existing regulations to give you that information since it is felt all ties with the past and the outside world must be broken, not gradually but at once."

"Listen," Johnny said desperately, "you must remember your own youth." He had tried every other verbal assault he could think of. Now he hardly thought flattery would work on the ancient bag of bones in front of him, but it seemed his last hope. "You must have had your lovers in your day, were you as attractive for your years as a younger woman…"

Something melted in the hag's eyes. She scrubbed her breastbone with the knuckles of one parchment hand, as if preening. "Why, yes," she admitted.

"I'm in love with this girl. You must know how I feel. He— he took her." At least in part, it was the truth. In love with Diane? He'd never thought of it, yet what had impelled him to battle Keleher in an uneven fight, to set out for New York when he could have ruled the encampment instead, to surrender himself to the Robots of the Citadel? Johnny smiled. Trying to awaken something in the hag, he had succeeded in awakening something, all right, but in himself.

"Such information I cannot give you, young man—"

"And I thought you remembered your youth!"

"—but they say the view from the corridor 13 exit is magnificent. To reach it, one travels along corridor 14, which is a dormitory for some of our young, unmarried women." The hag cackled. "Don't get caught."

"I won't. Thank you."

"Good luck, my boy." The hag patted his shoulder, crowed something which he failed to hear, and disappeared from the room.

Outside at a forking of four corridors, Johnny found a map and studied it. Lights recessed high on the walls showed him his direction, and soon he was pounding down the corridors and praying silently that the hag knew what she was talking about. By the time he reached corridor 14 he was breathless.

Several young women stood in the corridor talking. Their chatter was stilled when they saw Johnny, and those who had been in various stages of undress hastened to cover themselves. Clearly, it was not common for a man to venture this way, particularly at night.

"Are you lost?"

"No. I'm looking for someone. A girl named Diane."

They were smiling, and Johnny began to wonder. He suspected that corridor trysts were not particularly uncommon.

"Is she expecting you?" demanded the boldest of the women, who had stepped to the fore while her more timid companions drew back, ready to dart into the surrounding cubicles.

"I cannot truthfully say," Johnny admitted. "If she knew I was in the Citadel, I think she would be expecting me." But even that was with tongue in cheek, for ever since he had refused to fight with Starbuck, Diane had said not a word to him.

"This Diane, what does she look like?"

Johnny described her. When he finished, the woman chuckled. "Could you perhaps be trysting? From your description, I would say you love the girl, for no woman could be so beautiful. I think I know who you mean, though."

Still chuckling, the tall woman entered one of the cubicles while her companions melted away into the others. Soon Johnny stood alone in the corridor, waiting as nervously as a youth in Hamilton Village might wait while the village matchmaker entered a house to fetch him his bride. Someone appeared in the doorway. Not the tall woman. Diane!

"Johnny...Johnny Hope..."

"Diane, I never thought I would see you again. I thought Starbuck..."

"I was so afraid for you, because you couldn't adjust to your new life, because I thought you might do something desperate. I was a fool, I should have known why you refused to fight with Starbuck. Johnny, Johnny...let me look at you."

"Look later," he said, his eyes suddenly, unexpectedly misty. He drew her to him and for a long time stood there with her, feeling the beat of her heart tight against him, the warmth of her body and long smoothness of limbs. She was trembling, the warmth of her all a-flutter against him. She was murmuring something softly against his shoulder. He was whispering in her ear, "I love you. I love you, Diane…"

HER lips were perfumed and yielding, her arms went behind him, hands joining behind his neck, then playing with his hair. The Plague, his exile from Hamilton Village, the fight with Keleher, the long trek, even captivity in the Citadel—all were a small price to pay, he thought dreamily, then abruptly drew back.

"We don't want to stay here all our lives," he said.

"I'll go anywhere with you, Johnny."

"Save that for later, darling—but I love to hear it. I don't think we'd have much trouble leaving the Citadel."

"Not if we go tonight, we wouldn't. Every day I work with Starbuck, but if we left at once, now, tonight!"

Her newfound enthusiasm not only matched his, but added wings to it. He was on the point of saying yes, of leading her through the corridors in a dash for freedom, when he remembered. "We can't," he said. "Not tonight. We've got to include Amos Westler in our plan's."

"Westler is here?"

Johnny explained the situation to her, then added, "Tonight Westler went looking for some information about the Robots. He feels certain they have an Achilles Heel someplace, if only he can find it. Actually, it won't be easy dragging him away from the Citadel, even tomorrow night."

"We can wait one night longer, sweetheart. You convince him tomorrow."

"I don't like the thought of leaving you alone again until tomorrow night."

Diane stilled his words by placing cool fingers to his lips. "We have no choice. I can take care of myself one night more."

"Starbuck?"

"I can take care of myself in that respect, too. Go back to your dormitory and get some sleep."

"Tomorrow night. Same time, same place. Westler will be

with me."

They came close and drank of each other again. They parted, Johnny edging down the corridor backwards until the last shaft of light disappeared from the entrance to Diane's cubicle. His head was whirling in a giddy new delight, in a rapture that clouded his mind with a buoyant optimism that almost made him forget the Citadel, the Robots, and men like Harry Starbuck...

Footsteps pounding down the hall, heavy, too heavy for a woman's. Quickly Johnny flattened himself in the darkness of a niche that served some nameless purpose. With the light behind it, a shadow loomed, reared up toward him.

It was Harry Starbuck.

Johnny held his breath until the big man with the smug boy's face strode past. Heading for Diane? In all probability, yes. Follow him? Stop him? Attack him? Wild thoughts ran their course through Johnny's head. And lose everything, all they were looking forward to, for his impulsiveness? Footsteps receded. The shadow vanished. Even if he could follow Starbuck, overpower him and escape with Diane, their secret would be secret no longer, which would leave Amos Westler to fare for himself.

Wait for tomorrow, he told himself. His course seemed clear, yet he had to fight himself all the way back down the corridor until he had reached the male dormitories.

For many hours—which seemed like days—he waited up for Amos Westler, but his thoughts were all with Diane. If Starbuck so much as touched her...

CHAPTER EIGHT

"I FOUND it, Johnny! It was so obvious, it seems incredible no one has tried to end the Robot's reign before. But we can do it. One man could do it, alone. One man, with careful planning—"

"Diane is here, Amos. I saw her tonight. We're going to try

to break out tomorrow night, the three of us."

"You see," Westler went on, "there are two items of importance to consider. The first is Central Intelligence, the mind, the elan vital, the sentience that motivates the Robots. Did you know…could you ever imagine…that there was but one Central Intelligence for the entire Western Hemisphere? It seems incredible, but it's true. That was the Achilles Heel we sought, the seed of destruction that some pessimistic scientist had sown into the Robots in case man had created a Frankenstein."

"You didn't even hear what I said, did you? Tomorrow night, the three of us will be on our way out of here. I think we stand a good chance, Amos. If we—"

"The second item—" Westler cut in, then he did a slight double take. "Why…what in the world are you talking about? Escape? Now? You *can't* be serious. Right within our grasp is the chance to free humanity from a thraldom that it does not yet even fully recognize. Would you give up the chance to render the Robots harmless in exchange for your own personal safety?"

"Not mine…Diane's. We love each other, Amos. I can't imagine leaving her here for another moment that we don't have to. She's in…rather…we're *all* in grave danger every second we stay in this place. Just look about you. We're leaving tomorrow and we want you to come with us."

Westler paced back and forth, caged in spirit more than in body. "Look at you," he said, a trace of bitterness creeping into his voice. "You probably think of yourself as a responsible man. You think you're doing the right thing. But have you the right to the love of this woman when you're thinking only of tomorrow? Of one day out of thousands? Of one small life out of all that humanity has to offer? You want to hold this woman, to shower her with your affection, to show her your virility…is that it? While the rest of the human race goes to pot."

"That's enough, Amos," Johnny said in an icy tone. "My motives are my own. We leave here tomorrow."

"You're weak, Johnny," Westler said pointedly. "I pray

you're not a coward, too."

"Shut up, damn you."

Johnny couldn't deny all that Amos was saying, but he was a product of his own life's experiences. His parents had perished in the throws of a man-made Plague; he had been driven from his home, and he had even been rejected by the Shining Ones, too—until he had proved himself in battle. What did he owe to humanity, to that big, sprawling concept that took in all kinds of men and their women, children, good people, bad ones, big and small, with every type of mind and every type of body...?

"All right, go ahead and marry the girl. Do you think you'll raise a family? You and Diane are Shining Ones, Johnny. That's right...both of you. The rest of humanity fears you, and rightfully so. Your children will be cast out or even stoned if they venture near the villages of normal people. Perhaps life with the Robots would be best for them after all.

"But here...right now...we have the chance to stop all that. Not only could we negate the power of the Robots, but we could destroy the Plague as well. Do you hear me? We could destroy the Plague. Before you give me your final answer, let me tell you what I've found."

"I'm listening. But—"

"But nothing," the older man cut in, obviously exasperated. "Just listen carefully to everything I have to say...*please.*" Westler took a deep breath and continued in calmer voice. "Look, Johnny, the entity we've come to know as 'Central Intelligence' is essentially a vast cybernetics machine occupying an entire building—ironically, it's the United Nations building in old Manhattan where once were housed the dreams of all mankind. Now, what I've discovered is this...every Robot in North and South America has its own particular wavelength, although the master intelligence is in tune with all of them. Each individual Robot sentience is dependent for its existence upon the great cybernetics machines in Central Intelligence. In other words, if you were to destroy Central Intelligence, with that one, single blow you would literally 'kill' every Robot in the hemisphere."

"How did you find this out?"

WESTLER smiled. "There was one thing our Robot friends did not bargain for—an inquisitive ex-college professor like me! The information was available in—of all places—the main library right here in the city. It took some finding, but being an old hand at research I had an edge even on the Robots with their mechanical minds. Anyway, all you'd have to do is destroy Central Intelligence, and—"

"Might as well say destroy the moon, Amos. It's probably so well guarded a whole Army of men couldn't break through, let alone two."

"That's right," Westler said eagerly, "men could never hope to get through, but Robots could."

"What are you talking about?"

"I'm talking about the second thing I learned tonight. Once again, it was so deeply cross-referenced, so thoroughly hidden away that no one in the city apparently knew of its existence— probably not even the Robots. It's really not too surprising. The science of research has become such a dead thing here."

"But *you* found it," Johnny interjected.

"Yes," said the older man. "*I* found it. But now listen closely. The earliest model Robots were built to function in what might be described as a 'double fashion.' They were Robots, yes—but there were also compartments built inside them that a man could fit into for the purpose of controlling them manually. They were originally designed, you might say, as glorified suits of armor. While the research material is obviously quite old, all I could gather seems to indicate that no changes were ever made structurally to these early models. In other words, a man could still climb inside an older Robot today…right now…and no one would know the difference."

"You're forgetting one thing," Johnny pointed out. "Are you going to walk up to a Robot and tell him, 'Pardon me, my mechanical friend, I'd like to jump inside and use you as a disguise for a while?'"

"I'm not forgetting anything. But we work in the repair bays, remember? Think about it. We have full access to partially dismantled Robots. I'm certain we could find several older models, get them running again, and manage to get inside. Then we could make our way into Central Intelligence and..."

A thoughtful expression came over Johnny's face. "I still haven't said I'm going to do it. I'd like to help you, Amos. I'll take your word about the plan. It has possibilities. But that still has nothing to do with my own problems. Right now Diane is the most important thing."

"Johnny, you're being amazingly short-sighted. Diane's future, your future, all of our futures ultimately depend on this. Can't you understand it? You and I might very well determine whether mankind's future days are days of freedom...or slavery. Perhaps one man could do the job alone, but two would certainly have a better chance. So I need you to give me an answer, Johnny..."

"Let me think," said Johnny, waving Westler away when he would have continued talking. More quickly than he dared hope, he had found Diane. With equal swiftness, Westler had discovered what he sought. That left Johnny in the middle of a tug-of-war that wouldn't wait indefinitely for his answer.

AS THE closing gong sounded, 63-17-B watched the Shining Ones shuffle away from their benches and make their way down the corridor toward the cafeteria that would serve them an unimaginative but well-balanced evening meal. But two humans remained behind, talking avidly over the gleaming bodies of two stripped-down Robots. Strange, thought 63-17-B, who was now confronted with the first even mildly unusual event since taking over the dull routine of his new job that they should continue working after the closing gong had sounded. He could summon Hartness, the scarred human supervisor, and have him talk with the two. But no...he would do no such thing. If perhaps the humans were up to some mischief, and if it did not endanger

63-17-B's own position still further, then let them play. If it gave a few Robots and even Central Intelligence a hard time for a while, it served them right. Of course, nothing really serious could come from the tampering of two helpless humans…

"What about that guy up there?" Johnny raised an eyebrow in the direction of the supervising Robot, motionless on his stone perch. "Is he watching us?"

"It appears that he is. Unfortunately, we can't do a thing about it. At least not until we find out if these gadgets will work with us inside them. Here, Johnny—you see these tiny items? These are transistors, using germanium instead of a vacuum grid to activate electrons, smaller, more compact, more powerful, of longer life. Without them the whole science of cybernetics that ultimately made the Robots possible would never have advanced beyond the rudimentary stage. For with transistors replacing vacuum tubes you still need the entire U. N. building to house Central Intelligence. Under the older system, all New York City would not have been enough."

"Tell me later," Johnny pleaded. "I want to get started. The longer we delay here the longer it will take until we're finished. And I still have that appointment with Diane tonight. I couldn't contact her during the day because she said she works with Starbuck. We've got to hurry."

Westler's hands, guiding the complex tools, moved with swift efficiency, as if, indeed, he had worked with the Robots all his life. Wires were crossed, insulated, rearranged. Gaps and relays were tested and re-tested, gears changed, long-unused parts oiled, cleaned, checked for defects. Surface plates were clamped into place over layers of insulation. At last the two Robots lay there, supine but—Westler hoped—ready for human use.

"He's still watching," said Johnny.

"Let him. We couldn't prevent him. Only hope he suddenly doesn't decide to come down here for a closer look or send for help. It seems amazing he's done neither so far."

"Maybe he's asleep."

"Robots do not sleep. I assure you. Well, it's ready."

Westler reached into the Robots interior before clamping on the final head plates. Each Robot stood up in ponderous silence.

"You first, Johnny, I can clamp my plate from the inside. Are you sure my explanations on how to work this were satisfactory? Once inside we'll have to contact each other by signals only."

"What about the radio sets inside? I don't know much about radio, but you said they worked."

"They do, but the wavelength might be too close to a Robot wavelength and we'd give ourselves away. Remember, we are to be nothing more or less than two Robots once we climb inside. That way there shouldn't be any trouble. All ready? Up you go."

Johnny was boosted up, pulled himself within the cramped interior of the Robot. There was barely room for him to stand upright, his shoulders hunched, arms tight in front of him. A dizzying mass of dials and levers confronted him suddenly, and although Westler had explained them and diagrammed them and made Johnny memorize them, he was still bewildered by direct contact. He was almost afraid to try his first movement, lest the Robot remain immobile.

The faceplate slammed home. Johnny could see through the one-way plastic of the Robot's eyes as Westler climbed into his own machine.

Johnny pulled the starting lever and felt his Robot lurch forward. Must learn to control the motion...so...he was now aware of a lumbering gait, of a steady advance toward the farther wall...

Something made him whirl and peer through the rear eyes. The Robot supervisor was coming toward them at a rate of speed they couldn't match.

"YOU SEE?" said Starbuck proudly. "I am no longer a servant. I suppose you would call me a junior executive now. But I'm on the way up. Definitely on the way up. In a while there is no telling how far I can go."

"I'm sure of it," Diane nodded agreement. She didn't want to be bothered by Starbuck today, not when her thoughts were all on the night and Johnny. She was so nervous she couldn't keep from looking anxious. If only Starbuck, all wrapped up in himself the way he was, would fail to see it for a few hours longer.

"I suppose you wonder how I can advance so rapidly. It's quite simple, Diane. I look around me. I make contacts. I miss nothing. As an example, I even know of your meeting with Johnny Hope last night."

"What?"

"I wouldn't really mind it, except that my informant said you are considering escape from the Citadel. That, of course, is out of the question."

In his short time at the Citadel, Diane realized, Starbuck had affected a way of speaking that hardly fit his booming voice or boyish face. It was as if he had decided to ape the Shining Ones who stood highest in the Robots' confidence. To Diane it was contemptuous, although now her mind was awhirl with the thought that she and Johnny had been discovered.

"What are you going to do?" she asked in a small, helpless voice.

"Hope will be arrested. Naturally, he will never be permitted to see you again."

Diane stared at Starbuck in horror. Johnny must be found and warned. There was still time. They could alter their plans, this time in secrecy, without any women around who could spy on them for Starbuck. But she had to find Johnny before it was too late.

In sudden despair, she realized she didn't even know where to look.

CHAPTER NINE

STOP! Stand perfectly still.

The thought was unexpected, peremptory, driving into Johnny's brain with more authority than any words. He wanted to stop, wanted, to immobilize the Robot in which he hid—but where had the thought come from?

Westler's Robot was pointing a many-jointed metal arm at the supervising Robot that rushed toward them. Then, did the thought originate there? Could the Robot somehow send a soundless message to them?

Stop! Let me dismantle you.

The urge to render his own Robot motionless became stronger within Johnny. It was as if the unbidden thought originated outside his head but tried to direct his own muscles, as surely as his own mind.

Something made soft beeping noises in his ear and it took a while before he realized Westler wanted to break their radio silence, so soon after they had started. The other Robot was almost upon them.

Awkward and uncomfortable in his cramped quarters, Johnny found the radio switch and pulled it.

"We've got to destroy that Robot, Johnny. Now, at once, or we're finished."

"But how—"

The Robot was upon them, its unbidden thoughts stronger.

Halt...

It was Johnny who struck the first blow—clumsily, lifting his great right arm up and bringing it down stiffly on the other Robot's head. Metal arms came up, swung blurringly. A clanging tumult deafened Johnny as dents appeared inside the chamber of his own Robot's head. He triggered the levers mechanically now, aware that they were fighting under a tremendous disadvantage, for their fingers were still stiff on the unfamiliar controls and their artificial reflexes could not hope to match the Robot's.

"Look out, Johnny—"

Two metal shapes loomed, Westler and the real Robot. The three of them came together, clashing, clanging, metal arms swinging and wrecking metal bodies. It was Westler's Robot that went down first, slowly, buckling at the knee joints and then collapsing. Metal feet drove down upon it ponderously, crushing the head section. Westler's Robot was still.

Johnny hammered with huge metal hands at the other robot hardly knowing where he might strike a mortal blow. But the Robot slowed, its reactions grew feeble, its blows denting Johnny's head-chamber no longer. Finally, it sprawled across Westler's Robot, then rolled away and was still.

Cursing to himself, Johnny climbed down from his Robot, found the battered head plate of Westler's, and forced it open.

He saw at once he could never hope to extricate the older man, for the metal walls of his chamber had been crushed, knifing into bone and flesh and trapping him.

"Amos, can you hear me?"

THE eyelids fluttered opened with pain. "I never will see the end, Johnny…"

"What are you talking about?"

"Don't…fool me. I'm all broken, inside. I—"

"We'll get you out of there in no time."

"You'd have to melt…the metal down to…do it, and you know it."

"We'll do it." Your only hope is that the Robot did not have time to broadcast a warning. If…he did…you will have to hurry, but—"

"They still don't know our plans. Maybe they think we only want to escape, using these Robot bodies for a disguise."

"Perhaps. I hadn't thought…of that." Westler lapsed into silence, his face twisted with pain. "If you can do it, if you can destroy their cybernetics center...new start for humanity. I was going to tell you about the Plague, Johnny. The Robots...have been using...a particularly virulent form of the...toxin which does not exist naturally. Spreading it in the air, all over the earth. That, combined with the...toxin carried by a Shining One, causes illness...and death." Westler's words were harder to hear now, low, the barest whisper of sound. Johnny leaned close to the glazed eyes, the barely opening lips. "When the Robots are...gone...the Plague will die out almost at once. Shining Ones even will be harmless. You see why it's so important? You see..."

"I could never do it without you. We'll hide away somewhere, nurse you back to health—"

"Stop fooling...an old man. We both know I'm dying."

"That's ridiculous."

"Please...don't interrupt me. I want to finish telling you...the Robots communicate with humans by telepathy. You witnessed it yourself, a few...minutes ago. They can make it seem like your own thoughts and...who can say? Thought waves are electromagnetic, like...so many other things. There is nothing mysterious about...telepathy. Give humanity a chance to study what the...Robots have done and...you'll have civilization flourishing again within a generation. Give humanity the chance..." It was a whisper, a prayer.

On that final note of hope, Amos Westler died.

"THE human has emerged from the underground within his Robot and is heading northeast across the city."

"I still think we ought to stop him now, while we know we can do it."

"Silence. Think on the primary level. In unity we will triumph. It is our one weapon they cannot hope to match."

"But 63-17-B warned us before—he perished—"

"Precisely. That the humans were attempting something other than mere escape. We must find out what that is, what they have learned. Don't you realize that if this man fails another might succeed in his place? Whatever knowledge he has, perhaps it is widely disseminated. We must find out before we kill him."

There was a silence among the conclave of motionless Robots, their unblinking eyes intent upon a huge three-dimensional map of the city, following a tiny pip of light in its slow progress.

"He seems to be heading straight for Central Intelligence."

"That's hardly possible, unless it is mere coincidence."

"I don't think so…see? Not half a mile away, now."

"Have the supervisors discovered who is missing?"

"Yes. He was employed in the very repair bay where 63-17-B perished—a defective Robot, incidentally, and no great loss. We have given his name to the top level Shining Ones in the hope that they can help us."

"There is a Shining One, a human, here right now. He wants an audience concerning the rebel.

"Very well, although we'll have to make it brief."

Starbuck entered the chamber cockily, then lost his poise when he saw the solemn, unmoving conclave of Robots. "I have outside," he began, moistening his lips and talking rapidly, "a woman who this man, this Johnny Hope, loves. Can you understand me? Do you know what love is? He won't do a thing that might harm her."

We can understand.

"I thought that—"

We can read your thoughts. Leave your name with the Robot outside. Take this woman within the U. N. building and hold her there until you hear from us.

"The U. N. building?"

No questions. Go.

Starbuck shuffled from the room, self-conscious and fearful under the mental command.

"I doubt if we'll need the hostage, but you never can tell."

"It seems incredible that—"

"Does it? The man has almost reached the U. N. building.

It will take him perhaps half an hour, for the rubble is piled high there. Underground he could reach it in a few moments, but apparently he is unfamiliar with the passages."

"He has only recently arrived at the Citadel."

"Somehow, they have learned something. It is why we cannot kill the man until we are sure. Have them alerted at Central Intelligence, but let him enter. Watch him. If he blunders about as if he has arrived there by accident, kill him. If he knows something, take him alive."

"Someday we must learn the secret of Central Intelligence, if we are to survive. We must learn how to duplicate it or face the possibility of perishing in a single accident."

"Men built it once. Men could do it again."

"Defective! Silence. Man can do nothing we cannot do."

Then they were quiet, watching the tiny, darting blip on the three-dimensional map as it struggled through the uncleared rubble southwest of the U. N. building.

EVEN in ruin, the city held more wonders for Johnny Hope than he had ever thought possible. In many ways, it was like a scar on the face of the earth, pitted with bomb craters, strewn with the debris of toppled towers, its streets choked with fallen, crumbling masonry and blocked by the skeletons of buildings that once had stood, bare and rusted now but not always so, as monuments to the greatness of man. Yet it was a scar that could be healed, a broken, dying city which could be made great again, with men and women roving its streets, repairing the structures, making the living city function once more.

That was Amos Westler's dream. It was the dream of all mankind, Johnny thought philosophically, although they did not realize it as they roved the earth in hunter-bands of Shining Ones or tilled its soil in small communities fearful of the Plague.

Now, directly ahead of him, he could see the monolithic slab of the U. N. building. Like one structure in five, it stood incredibly intact, a remembrance of the past and a promise of the future. We can build again, Johnny thought, without the

Robots and the Plague. They could build again or they would die. Natural world or artificial world—men or Robots—they could not survive jointly.

Battered and broken but still functioning adequately, Johnny's Robot pushed through the debris south of the U. N. building to the edge of the river. He stood there a moment and stared upstream at the gaunt ruins of a bridge, now tumbled down the river and resting on the river-bottom, thrusting its towers up beyond the surface of the water and toward the sky. Men had used that bridge once, long ago but within the memory of Johnny's father, to reach the country beyond. The bridge might be rebuilt. Men might learn to use it again. It was as if, in dying, Amos Westler had transferred his own vision to Johnny, showing him a dream of the unborn tomorrow—its birth or stillborn death depending entirely upon Johnny's success or failure today.

Half a dozen Robots stood about the wide terrace leading to the building, but Johnny ignored them, for he had passed many in the broken streets of the city and grown accustomed to them. He entered the building through a door of glass and metal and was not aware of the Robots entering it behind him.

His impulse was to climb down from his Robot, to stretch his cramped arms and legs and find something to eat, then explore the wonders of this new place. Above his head, the ceiling was high and vaulted. Ramps led away, curving and graceful, in all directions and he longed to feel his feet, his own feet, upon them, and to explore until he satiated himself with this wonder and sought another.

To leave the Robot would be suicide. Had the thought been his own—or a metal-made thought, instilled in him some unknown way, an unbidden suicide thought? It was less specific than the commands of the Robot that had perished in the repair bay, but Johnny guessed it came from outside nevertheless.

He advanced mechanically, for Westler had given him careful directions. The ramps led up, higher and higher, past the rooms in which men from many lands once, long ago, used to debate their future—then higher still, climbing...

There was noise behind him. He whirled in cramped quarters, peered from the Robot's second set of eyes. A dozen Robots climbed the ramp behind him, gaining. He let his mind drift blankly, let their thoughts reach him.

He is not wandering aimlessly.

Somehow he learned. He learned.

Capture him.

HE ran now, awkwardly, his own Robot not smooth and graceful, a flawless piece of machinery like the others. He clomped and clattered up the ramp and prayed for time.

The ramp soared upward, curved to the left. Once he looked down at the floor of the rotunda so far below and became giddy with the distance and the thought of falling; He leaned over the railing and looked. His head whirled...

At the last moment, he drew his Robot back from the edge, stabbing half-blindly at the controls that propelled it. They had almost driven him to suicide. He must keep his mind a perfect blank—or, better still, think of something that would keep them at bay. Diane, his love for her—Diane...

A Robot waited for him at the top of the ramp. Those behind him were gaining rapidly, driving death wishes deep within his brain.

The Robot above him abruptly swung into motion, but Johnny desperately sidestepped the lunge that would have sent him hurtling to the floor of the rotunda. The other Robot checked its own inertia and came for Johnny again, huge arms swinging, trying to crush him within the metal chamber as Amos Westler had been crushed. Johnny parried the blows with his own metal arms, then reached out and heard machinery groan within his metal frame as he lifted the other Robot and hurled it in the path of his pursuers.

There was a grinding, clattering crash of metal. Johnny saw three forms detach themselves from the arcing ramp and tumble, swinging and twisting in air grotesquely, to the floor, where they struck resoundingly and broke apart, the metal arms and legs flying.

Then he was climbing again, the remaining Robots far below him and disorganized now. But soon, he knew, they would be capable of following.

It was as Amos Westler had predicted. After a time, the ramp grew smaller. It no longer climbed now—it had soared high and now was just below the girdered ceiling. It was hardly wide enough for Johnny's Robot, it shook dangerously with the tread of metal feet. Here, Johnny knew, was the sanctuary. This was the Achilles Heel. This was the entrance, this ramp that no Robot could traverse. Here the way led to self-functioning, self-repairing machinery, to Central Intelligence. Here was man's final hope in the eyes of the original inventor. Here was the guarantee that the Robots, if they became some Frankenstein monster, could be met and conquered.

For no Robot could guard the final portal to Central Intelligence. No Robot could even draw close enough to alter the thin ramp. Johnny smiled grimly as comprehension grew. If Robots could become neurotic, this was the place for it. They could have employed their human servants, the Shining Ones, to alter the place, but would have divulged their secret in the process.

Still smiling, Johnny halted his Robot, opened the faceplate clumsily from the inside, and climbed out. He sat on the ramp and flexed stiff arms and legs, then stood up and heard the Robots below him. He could see them now, no longer advancing, milling about in confusion. Their weight would destroy the ramp, and they knew it. They could never hope to reach him.

It was all so incredibly simple.

Was it?

One Robot had been above him.

Then they knew he was coming. What had they prepared for him beyond the point where the Robots could not climb? Shrugging, he advanced warily.

Soon he could see where the ramp reached a small doorway, much too low and narrow to admit a Robot, even if one of the machines could have climbed the ramp this far.

"Hold it, Johnny. Don't come any closer."

STARTLED, he looked up. Harry Starbuck stood in the doorway, holding Diane in front of him.

"I'm not fooling, Hope. If you come any closer I'll throw her off. It's a long way down."

"You're crazy, Starbuck. You'll never leave this place alive." But even as he spoke, he knew he could never reason with the man. "The Robots can't let you carry their secret from here. Your only hope is to cooperate with me."

"Is that so? They're sending some more men up to get you. All I have to do is hold the fort until...cut it out, Hope! Stay right there." Starbuck edged out of the doorway, dragging Diane along with him to the railing at one side of the ramp. "I'll do it if you make me."

"Don't listen to him, Johnny! I'm not afraid." Hair disheveled, clothing torn, face bruised, she still looked beautiful to him. All at once she stood for everything Westler had mentioned: for the future of man, for the dreams of tomorrow, for a free world with no Plague and no Robots. But for Westler the choice would have been easy. The girl— or humanity.

Westler had not been in love. Now Starbuck had forced Diane, back arched, breasts thrust forward, out over the railing. She struggled in his grip, but futilely. He could hurl her out over the edge and into space if he wished.

"Back up, Hope. I want you to go back down the ramp and surrender to the Robots. You're only delaying things. More men will be here soon. You're licked and you know it."

Wearily, Johnny retreated. "Don't hurt her," he said. "Promise me that."

"You crazy? I want her for myself."

The thought numbed Johnny. He hadn't considered it that way. A live Diane or a dead one was one thing. But a Diane forced to submit to Starbuck...

He reached his own immobile Robot, saw the others, not twenty yards below him, waiting, thought he heard shouts somewhere behind them. He must do what he had come to do as if Diane did not exist. It was Starbuck who had made the choice for him.

But there was a wild possibility...

Quickly, he climbed within his Robot, activated it, lumbered forward. He could feel the ramp shaking with each step he took. At any moment, its struts might collapse and send him hurtling to his death, trapped in his man-shaped metal coffin, far below.

Soon he could see Starbuck again, on the ramp outside the doorway, holding Diane. Starbuck's eyes went wide. Starbuck frowned, then began to lick his lips anxiously.

"You can't come up here!" he cried, not knowing Johnny was inside. "The ramp won't hold you. I sent the man down to surrender, anyway. Do you have him? Is he dead? What do you want, anyway? I can come down myself. Don't come any closer, not unless you want the ramp to collapse. Keep away— do you hear me?"

Johnny advanced slowly, the ramp shaking with each stride no longer, but dipping and rocking constantly now, almost ready to go. Starbuck retreated, taking Diane with him. Through the doorway they went—

Out fell the faceplate of Johnny's Robot. He tumbled after it as the ramp shook, metal grinding against metal, then snapped. He leaped forward as the ramp caved in. He felt his feet shoot out from under him, saw metal dropping away, twisting, to his left. He clawed out with his hands, gripped a jagged edge, pulled himself up slowly as blood made his hands slip.

He stood in what was left of the doorway, trembling as reaction set in, his heels on the brink of nothing, his bloodied hands aching.

Starbuck roared and charged at him, attempting to drive him back a few inches to his death. But Johnny caught him, met him halfway with no room to evade the charge, and they grappled there, teetering on the edge.

"You tricked me," Starbuck moaned. "That Robot... you were inside."

A KNEE blurred up at Johnny, exploding in violent pain. He felt himself falling and managed to twist away from the edge of the sundered ramp. He hit the floor with waves of nausea boiling up from his stomach. He lay there, blinking his eyes.

Starbuck came for him.

He drew his legs up instinctively, the knees bent, then straightened as Starbuck leaned over him. His feet caught the big man squarely on the chest, lifted him, pushed—

Starbuck went over the edge of the ramp, screaming all the way down.

Inside, Johnny found Diane, dazed, on the floor. He ignored her. She could wait, for now he was a man possessed. The machinery, which he could never hope to understand, was all about him bank on bank of it lining the walls, humming with its strange, sentient energy, glowing and flickering with a million lights.

Kill yourself.

Two words, clamoring, insistent, inside his skull. Their final hope... He felt himself edging back toward the doorway, and the death that awaited him just outside. He looked at Diane, huddled on the floor, her lips parted—Johnny..."

I love you, he thought. The words of death and those of life and hope fought inside his skull, twisting his brain, battling there for mastery...

He found something, a length of metal rod. He ripped it loose and began to attack the machinery he would never understand. He was a wild man. The strength flowed in from elsewhere, raising his arm, swinging it high over his head and down. Sparks flew as his metal club battered the crystalline tubes, the delicate wiring, the metal cases. Glass shattered, sprinkled him, brought blood from a dozen cuts on his face. Electricity hummed, then shrieked, then wailed off distantly on a register too high for his ears.

Raise his arm and plunge...lift it and bring it down, battering, the metal club part of him...

It was Diane who eased the twisted rod from his fingers, soothed him with her words. "It's finished. Easy, Johnny. You've done it."

The place was a shambles. Bank on bank of gutted machinery lay silent there, on a floor strewn with glass, with wire, with filaments, with nameless things that were the brains for a million Robots.

"There's another way out, Johnny. Starbuck took me here. Behind that wall, you—"

She took his hand and they went. The passage was dark and cool and smelled musty, as if air did not circulate very well within it. It was a place for thinking and dreaming of tomorrow. It was a place for realizing you could go back to the hills and find Keleher and his Shining Ones and convince them they should at least look at the City, the City that belonged to them now, to them and DeReggio and his villagers—and all the others. And there must be a coming together of Keleher and DeReggio, with Johnny as mediator, and a realization that the last Plague victim had been smitten and humanity had a long path to travel but that it could set foot upon it right now, at once.

Outside, it was beginning to grow dark, but Johnny could make out the still forms of the Robots, gleaming red with final sunlight, sprawled up and down the broken streets. The Shining Ones within the City stalked about furtively in small groups, not yet knowing what it meant to live without their masters. Perhaps in time Keleher and all the others could teach them.

"Hungry?" said Johnny. "We could stop and eat."

"No. You?"

"In a different way."

They followed the last slanting rays of the sun to the western river and the mainland beyond it.

THE END

If you've enjoyed this book, you will not want to miss these terrific titles…

ARMCHAIR SCI-FI & HORROR DOUBLE NOVELS, $12.95 each

D-21 **EMPIRE OF EVIL** by Robert Arnette
THE SIGN OF THE TIGER by Alan E. Nourse & J. A. Meyer

D-22 **OPERATION SQUARE PEG** by Frank Belknap Long
ENCHANTRESS OF VENUS by Leigh Brackett

D-23 **THE LIFE WATCH** by Lester del Rey
CREATURES OF THE ABYSS by Murray Leinster

D-24 **LEGION OF LAZARUS** by Edmond Hamilton
STAR HUNTER by Andre Norton

D-25 **EMPIRE OF WOMEN** by John Fletcher
ONE OF OUR CITIES IS MISSING by Irving Cox

D-26 **THE WRONG SIDE OF PARADISE** by Raymond F. Jones
THE INVOLUNTARY IMMORTALS by Rog Phillips

D-27 **EARTH QUARTER** by Damon Knight
ENVOY TO NEW WORLDS by Keith Laumer

D-28 **SLAVES TO THE METAL HORDE** by Milton Lesser
HUNTERS OUT OF TIME by Joseph E. Kelleam

D-29 **RX JUPITER SAVE US** by Ward Moore
BEWARE THE USURPERS by Geoff St. Reynard

D-30 **SECRET OF THE SERPENT** by Don Wilcox
CRUSADE ACROSS THE VOID by Dwight V. Swain

ARMCHAIR SCIENCE FICTION CLASSICS, $12.95 each

C-7 **THE SHAVER MYSTERY, Book One**
by Richard S. Shaver

C-8 **THE SHAVER MYSTERY, Book Two**
by Richard S. Shaver

C-9 **MURDER IN SPACE**
by David V. Reed

ARMCHAIR MASTERS OF SCIENCE FICTION SERIES, $16.95 each

M-3 **MASTERS OF SCIENCE FICTION, Vol. Three**
Robert Sheckley, "The Perfect Woman" and other tales

M-4 **MASTERS OF SCIENCE FICTION, Vol. Four**
Mack Reynolds, "Stowaway" and other tales

AN UNDERGROUND ADVENTURE TO REMEMBER

After being catapulted to mysterious caverns deep within the bowels of the Earth and promptly named, "Nors-King," adventurer Jack Odin experienced a dramatic undertaking of unusual depth and scope, including his bewitchment by a statuesque princess of the royal house, as well as having to safeguard against the destructive desires of a mad prince.

Follow along as Odin encounters a variety of strange creatures, including breath-taking beauties, mysterious dwarves, and vicious beasts. They are the very personifications of myth that men of the surface world had so long ago disposed of as impossible and unreal, but they are all very palpable in the world into which Jack Odin has been thrust…

CAST OF CHARACTERS

DR. JACK ODIN
Adrift and alone in his world, he had no purpose… Would he be the unlikely hero needed to save another?

MAYA
The beautiful, golden-eyed Princess of the Bron, her determination to preserve her people was unmatched.

GRIM HAGEN
A hot-headed murderer, the Prince of the Bron. His only true desire was…destruction!

JUL
An elder who was held in high regard, would his convictions be enough to encourage needed change in his crumbling world?

WOLDEN
How far would this scientist and philosopher go to preserve and defend the many treasures in his world?

GUNNAR
A loyal and noble warrior of the Neebling. His fearsome strength and force of will could not be discouraged!

WHITE OWL
No more than four feet in stature with very little to say, he was a brutal fighter to the end.

HUNTERS
OUT OF TIME

By
JOSEPH E. KELLEAM

ARMCHAIR FICTION
PO Box 4369, Medford, Oregon   97501-0168

*For more information about Armchair Books and products, visit our
website at…*

www.armchairfiction.com

Or email us at…

armchairfiction@yahoo.com

CHAPTER ONE

IT WAS only a dream, he thought. A bubble rising up from memories of the past. Doctor Jack Odin half-opened one eye, glanced at the bedroom window where a gray October morning was breaking. Then he closed his eyes again and tried to go back to sleep.

What was the dream? Maybe he could pick it up again. There was something about it that made him recall those bright days when he was a boy; and his father, home from work, would take him on his knee and read such delightful, glittering poems and stories in a deep, magical voice that the little boy thought was beyond compare. Still, there was something troubling about the dream.

He had been visited by a strange little man, dressed a bit like Robin Hood, wearing a peaked red cap into which a single white feather had been thrust jauntily.

Then he remembered the poem that he and his father had loved:

"Up the airy mountain,
  Down the rushy glen,
  We daren't go a-hunting
  For fear of little men;
  Wee folk, good folk,
  Tramping all together;
  Green jacket, red cap,
  *And white owl's feather."**

So that was it. A few lines of a poem. Lost out of time and looking in vain for the little boy who had chanted them at play. Then Dr. Jack Odin opened both eyes with a start,

----

* The Fairies by William Allingham.

remembering that there was a shadow at the window.

Throwing his cover aside, he leaped out of bed, glad that he had a prowler to break the awful boredom that had enveloped him these past months.

HUNTERS OUT OF TIME

By Joseph E. Kelleam

On the beach the dwarfs slashed fiercely at the blood-curdling monstrosities
that came out of the deep to attack them.

But the prowler appeared to be more startled than Odin. His head and shoulders were showing above the windowsill. He wore a tight-fitting, laced jacket, and on his head was a scarlet, peaked cap into which one white feather was thrust at a jaunty angle. His pointed chin and wide-apart eyes gave him a gnomish look, although the wide shoulders and strong, gnarled hands by which he was clinging easily to a second-story window dispersed any idea of fragility.

As Jack started out of bed the little man's eyes opened wide and he lowered himself from sight. Jack thought he could hear him clambering down the drainpipe. Rushing to the window he caught a glimpse of a tiny figure, not over four feet high, that ran across the misty lawn and dived into the shadows of a hedge.

Well, there was no use trying to sleep now. He smoked a couple of cigarettes, bathed and dressed, and went downstairs for breakfast.

Mrs. Forgan, his father's old housekeeper, was in the kitchen. Mr. Forgan was dozing by the stove. Of late he moved from place to place, as his wife directed, and then promptly went to sleep.

Mrs. Forgan, who had practically reared Jack Odin, gave him a cheery good morning, and turned on the kitchen radio. Forgan opened one eye, blinked twice, and nodded.

A Washington announcer was giving the news: "—and this is the story of the murder of General Mathew, our Chief of Staff. His guest, a tall, lean, dark man, arrived at the General's house last night about nine o'clock. Apparently he had an appointment. The General's secretary let the visitor in and brought him to the General's study. The General closed the door after them. The study is soundproof, and nothing was heard between then and midnight. At that time, the secretary became alarmed and called the butler. They crashed through the locked door to find the General stabbed to death. The visitor had fled through an open window. Evidently the General had defended himself with an old dagger which he always kept on his desk for a letter-opener. This bloodstained dagger was found near the General's body.

Bloodstains were also found upon the window. The assailant, doubtless, was wounded. A taxi-driver has stated that he saw a man answering the visitor's description speeding toward the Baltimore Road. He thinks there were others in the car—" And on and on. There had been little news lately. The announcer was making the most of it. Opinions of police officers, investigators, and Army officials were repeated. Mere theory, at this time, although a search of the General's private papers as well as a statement by his secretary hinted that the General, always a close-mouthed man, had been working on something *big*.

Breakfast over, Jack Odin went out into the old-fashioned yard which still boasted cast-iron hitching posts along the drive. But a thin, cold mist was falling, and after walking about the square-built, two-story house for a few minutes he returned to his study. As he closed the door to the front porch behind him, he could hear the sound of sirens screaming along the Baltimore Road. The hue and cry for the escaped killer was on. For a moment he felt a tinge of sympathy for the hunted man. In that long retreat from the Yalu he had known what it was to be cold, wounded—and hunted. The weary haunted feeling of having to run and keep running.

The day passed slowly. Just as Jack had spent so many days during the past year, he wandered from room to room, alternately listening to TV and the radio, thumbing through his books, then he wrote a couple of letters, and grew so moody that even his parents' old clock on the mantelpiece of his study seemed to be striking off the seconds on an anvil.

He breathed a sigh of relief when the last bit of daylight faded from the windows. At supper Mrs. Forgan warned him: "Jack, you're mooning around too much. What you need is a wife. One of them frivolous, expensive ones. You're getting old before your time."

Pete Forgan raised one eyelid and his chin enough to grumble: "Yeah, boy, you're in a rut six feet deep. You need a wife, but not one of them ordinary ones. Get you a wife who's lively—and—uh—different." Then he fell asleep at the table and snored until Mrs. Forgan roused him and sent him off to bed.

Mrs. Forgan cleared the dishes away, puttered a bit around the kitchen, and soon followed her husband. Jack Odin retired to his study.

The big house was old. The tall sycamores were losing the last of their leaves as the first gusts of October tore across the old-fashioned grounds where four generations of Odins had played. The mist was sweeping away and a yellow moon was soaring across the sky as racks of clouds scudded before it. The leaves went rattling and scraping across the yard and fluttered against the old window screens and clung there shivering until the boisterous wind caught them and sent them dancing over the roof, sliding and skittering against the time-worn, uneven shingles.

Young Doctor Jack Odin stood at the window of his old-fashioned library and looked out at the thick clumps of shrubs and shadows. The moon sailed in and out of the clouds. The grounds had a mournful, graveyard look about them, and the rising wind was playing a dirge upon the emptying branches of the trees. It was a lonely night and a depressing one. The wind, sweeping so much of summer's splendor away, reminded him that it was not a pleasant thing to be the last of the Odins. A doctor, he was in a better position to analyze the feeling than most men. But it defied him. All day he had wandered morosely about the big barn of a house. It was a feeling that all was not well with him, that the Grey Spinners were taking up the threads of his life after allowing them to lie idle for over a year and were toying with the faintest idea of a new pattern.

Still, he was in no mood for medicine or analysis either. All that day he had been wondering why he, a Golden Gloves and fencing champion, had spent eight hard years studying medicine and another four with the United States Air Force to prove to himself that as far as he was concerned his chosen profession was dull. Toward the end of the Korean affair he had seen enough proof of what a burp-gun can do to leave no illusion of glamour or excitement to war. His uniform had been hanging in a closet upstairs for over a year and he had forgotten to put mothballs in its pockets.

Turning away from the window he selected a book at random and sat down at an old ebony table which had been his father's delight. After adjusting a reading lamp he turned the pages slowly, not reading a word, wondering what life was all about and what in thunder he was going to do with his own. Fortunately, he thought, there was a great deal of money to his account in banks in the District and Baltimore. Finding a job was not a necessity.

There was a saying in the neighborhood that the Odin luck was either very good or very bad. Jack Odin's family could trace itself no farther back than to old Simon Odin who had tired of being a peddler in Baltimore and made a comfortable fortune by operating a way-station in the Underground Railway. While his descendants were proud of him, they had to admit that Old Simon had certainly not conducted his business for purely humanitarian purposes. The old man had built this big comfortable house not far from Belin and spent his closing years on various commissions in Washington. It became a tradition in the family that the men served the government in one way or another, though none had risen any higher than an assistant-secretaryship. While the Odins claimed Maryland as their home, they were more closely associated with the District.

One Odin had been an aide to General Lew Wallace and a distant relative had died with Custer, but all in all they had been a prosaic lot, serving various departments faithfully but not brilliantly. Always managing to add a bit to Old Simon's fortune. Honest, in their way, faithful, but—Young Doctor Jack Odin had to admit—shrewd as any peddler.

His mother had died when he was three. Jack's father, the last of the old-line Odins, died a month before the Korean affair was over. After his hitch with the Air Force, Dr. Odin came back to his home to moss over. A hundred-year-old trust firm settled the estate so capably that he had spent little more than ten minutes time with it.

So for the past year, he had dawdled about the house, now and then looking at his diploma. In the past month he had spoken to no one save the Forgans.

Tired of the book, Jack Odin opened the table drawer and got out some stationery and a pen. He had been putting off a letter to an old Air Force acquaintance in Kansas for two months. He scribbled for a time, listening to the morning wind. Finally he tore up the page in disgust. Taking up a fresh sheet he began scrawling and drawing upon it. Scarcely thinking, he wrote down any words and phrases that came to his mind. It was a trick of relaxation that he had learned while in uniform.

But, suddenly, his mind came awake again. There, in the middle of the page, he had written the same phrase that had come to him when first awaking that morning:

"White Owl Feather—"

Damn, he thought to himself, doctors can get more neurotic than their patients if they don't watch out. There was no sense in saying that the words had no significance, but the question was this: Had he dreamed about White Owl

Feather?

A little man with a white feather in his cap. Doctor Jack Odin could not make up his mind whether he had dreamed the whole affair or whether some screw had worked loose in his brain. He had a fair knowledge of psychiatry. Sometimes a forgotten memory could raise the very devil with a lonely man. All day long the poem that had been a favorite of his childhood had kept singing in his head:

> *"Up the airy mountain,*
> *Down the rushy glen,*
> *We daren't go a-hunting*
> *For fear of little men;*
> *Wee folk, good folk,*
> *Tramping all together;*
> *Green jacket, red cap,*
> *And white owl's feather."*

He threw his pen across the room. "Another month of this loafing and I'll be afraid of my shadow. Hang it all, I'll re-enlist tomorrow."

Then Jack looked up at the window and there they were. Three of them. Three little men with wide eyes, pointed chins and ears. Each of them wore a Robin Hood's cap and in each cap was a feather. White Owl Feather, his visitor of the morning, was in the center. All three had an owlish look and they were staring at him—not in fear, but as though they were appraising him.

As he stared back they slowly moved away from the window. They spoke a few words to each other in a language he had never heard.

He thought he heard other voices. One, he fancied, was a woman's. Low and musical, with just a breath of fear

96

hovering over the syllables.

There were steps upon the front porch and a low, insistent rapping at the door. Wondering and still bewildered by the turn that the night was taking, he went through the house to the living room, turned on the lights and opened the door.

Without further invitation they came in. First, a grotesque broad-shouldered little man carrying one end of a stretcher. Then the stretcher itself. Upon it and nearly covered by a dirty quilt was a long thin man. He was young. His face was dark and his eyes were closed. Had he not suddenly moved in pain Jack Odin might have thought him dead. White Owl Feather was carrying the other end of the stretcher. Behind him came the third little man, the least of all, white-haired and stooped, not over three feet high, his face lined with worry and something else—was it compassion, pity, or contempt? Odin could not tell.

And last came the girl. Nearly five-feet-five, bareheaded and sandaled, her dark curly hair had a tinge of red to it, and it sparkled with a few silver drops of mist. Thin and lithe, she stood at the door, looking at him with inquisitive, golden eyes. Clad in a tight-fitting scarlet robe that was belted with a white sash, she stood straight and proud. There in the night, her breasts high and full, she looked to Jack Odin like a queen who might have stepped down from the pictured wall of some Pharaoh's tomb. Or, and this was a better comparison, a goddess of those strange people of Crete, come back to look at the world with wonder in her golden eyes, and to take up life where Crete and her far-flung galleys had left it so long ago.

She seemed to be the spokesman for the odd group. The little white-haired gnome closed the door behind them. The three dwarfs looked at the girl and waited. She hesitated, studying Odin's face, her mouth pursed, a thin little line of concentration forming itself across her high forehead. As though she was trying to shape her words carefully in a language that she did not altogether understand.

The dark, thin man upon the stretcher moved in pain and a groan escaped from his set jaws.

Then she spoke. There was the faintest trace of an accent in her voice. Still, it was musical and not hesitant at all.

"You are a doctor?" she asked.

"Not a practicing one, Miss. I was more of a soldier than a doctor. Now I have given up both professions. This man needs attention. Judging from the color of his face and all the blood on the quilt I would say he needs a transfusion. I recommend a hospital—"

"There is no time for what you call a hospital. He is strong. Also, something of a fool. Foolish and strong enough to live. He has been stabbed in the chest. I myself could stop the blood if I had the proper instruments."

The one Jack Odin had called White Owl Feather shuffled his feet and spoke a few words to the girl in the same language that Odin had heard from his study.

She answered with one sharp syllable. Plainly, it meant "Quiet" or even "Shut up."

"What did he say?" Odin inquired.

"He says you are a man who is not sure of himself. Like a man who stands at a crossroads and hopes that the wind will turn him one way or the other, for he cannot make up his mind which way to go."

Odin laughed. "Then he is something of a psychologist. For I am that man. Still, I don't like to be reminded of such by uninvited guests. Suppose I tell the five of you to get the hell out of here?"

Golden eyes flashed. The dark, regal head went even higher. He expected her to stamp her feet. But she stood tall and still, except for the rising and falling of her high breasts beneath the tight robe of silky scarlet.

"He is more than a psychologist. All the Neeblings have insight into the hearts of men. Still, even I can tell that you are wavering like smoke in the wind. Are you a coward? A man who has been both a soldier and a doctor should be able to stop the blood. This one is still bleeding. In time—"

With a faint shrug of her bare shoulders she rested her case.

"But I have no license to practice medicine in this state. You see, I went straight from med school into the Air Force—"

"Foolishness," she answered scornfully. "One is either a doctor or one isn't. This thing called 'a license' I don't understand." And she added a few words in her own language that made the three dwarfs smile.

Oh well, Jack Odin thought, the decision would have to be his. Why waste words arguing with this strange girl. Anyway, there was something exciting about the five—something exhilarating about this girl. He laughed and caught himself. Odd! He could not remember when he had laughed. The Korean War, the indecision about his profession, the loss of his father who had been such a pal in the old days, all these had stolen the laughter from him.

"Take him into my study there. You'll find a long table. Throw the books on the floor and put him on it. I'll find my bags and get some hot water."

Thirty minutes later Doctor Jack Odin looked up from his patient and nodded to the four onlookers with an unprofessional air. "He'll do," he said—and hoped that he was right.

The lean, dark man lay upon the table with jaws clenched. Only once had he opened his eyes while Odin was at work. Then he had given the doctor one dark scowl, filled with venomous hatred, and had spoken a few words in that strange language. Odin hadn't the slightest idea what the man was saying, but he knew he was cursing him. He had already developed a distaste for the whole business and a hearty dislike for the patient. He had a knife wound, he guessed. A nasty gash, which ran almost from the left shoulder, zigzagging down across the chest and ending in the splintered lower rib on the right side which had stopped the force of the blow. No accident this, Odin thought. A knife—probably a dull knife wielded by a powerful man.

Anyway, the lean man had guts. Not a sound from him, hardly a wince of pain though Odin must have hurt him plenty.

The girl and the three owlish dwarfs stared at him. Good God, Odin thought, after all I've done for this crew they're looking at me as though I was the sorriest bungler.

It was true. For all her regal look, the girl's eyes held a bit of sympathy—for Odin, not the patient. And the dwarfs wore a doubtful expression as though they were wondering if they had not come to the wrong place.

"I still think he needs a transfusion," Odin advised. Then he added cautiously: "This will leave a bad scar, you know."

She brushed a dark curl from her high forehead. "Serves him right. Jul, see what you can do."

The smallest, oldest dwarf came forward and placed his fingertips on the lean man's forehead, then slowly drew them back across the temples to the nape of the neck. Again and again. And all the while the bent little man was whispering a low voiced chant that had a soothing, calming sound in its repeated syllables.

Odin had not realized how old the little man was. His hair, which brushed his shoulders, was white. His face had the white fragility about it of very old china. His eyes, the palest blue, peered from under bushy white eyebrows with an intense farsighted stare as though they had seen too much. And yet, in that same stare was a mingling of both compassion and indifference.

Odin turned his gaze from the old man to the two others. White Feather was nearly a foot taller, with muscular arms and shoulders. Both men wore green short-sleeved jackets, which were tight-fitting and laced across the front.

The third dwarf was the largest of the three. He stood nearly an inch short of five feet. But while the old man had that look of porcelain fragility and White Owl Feather had an elfin air about him, the last of the three was muscled like a wrestler. His measurement around the shoulders must have been as much as his height. He wore a single red feather in his cap. His chest seemed to be bursting from the tight jacket, and his waist, belted and buckled with a two-inch square of gold, was remarkably small. His powerful, long arms matched the big chest and shoulders. His chin was not so pointed as his fellows, and his broad face was solid and strong. In spite of his height, he had the look of a fighting man. One who would not anger easily, but after beginning a charge would not stop until he reached his goal.

The girl saw Odin studying the broad-shouldered dwarf. "He is called Gunnar," she told him. "You have heard the name of Jul. The middle one is White Owl. I am called Maya." She sighed. "It has been a long night. We had better go now. Thanks to you, Doctor. I do not know your name. In my country a host usually introduces himself."

Odin flushed. The girl scored hard when she struck. "The name is Odin. Doctor Jack Odin, if you wish. Or Captain Jack Odin. It does not matter. Besides, I am not your host remember. You invited yourselves. I wish you hadn't—"

One look at the lithe brunette before him assured him that he was lying. This night was worth a score of those he had lately seen.

Far away a siren screamed and faded into the east.

Jul was growing uneasy. He and the girl fell to talking excitedly in that strange language of theirs which to Odin seemed both alien and familiar.

"We will go now." She turned to Odin. "I will not offer you money, though it seems to be the ruling custom in this country. Our thanks to you, Jack Odin. He," she swept her hand toward Jul, "wants you to accept something. He says that no good will come of this night. He says it will keep us from forgetting you when you are in trouble. We should be able to remember you for yourself, I am thinking. Still, his token is worth much. It would take the rest of the night for me to tell you how much it is worth—"

Jack Odin was thinking that he could think of no better way to spend the rest of the night than to listen to this exotic girl. The way she held her head high, the way she shrugged her shoulders, the way she tossed her dark curls—

As though sensing his thoughts she paused and looked down at her sandals. "You must believe me. If trouble comes, and Jul says it will, you must keep the token."

At this moment the old man took a gleaming object from beneath his jacket and handed it to Odin without further ceremony.

Odin turned the token over in his hand. It was a key of ivory, about four inches long, deeply slotted. Each slot was inlaid with red jewels—rubies, he wondered, though he knew little about precious stones.

He turned it over in his hands for a second, then thrust it into his pocket and bowed to the old man.

From the stretcher came a yowl of protest. Almost like the screech of a hurt cat.

The patient, his dark face tinged with blue, was trying to

lift himself to his elbows. From his narrow, bloodless lips came a torrent of words. Cursing and protesting he tried to get to his feet.

Then Jul thrust him down and began that curious stroking from temple to nape, crooning softly all the while. In less than a minute the patient collapsed weakly. In another minute he was asleep.

Jul motioned. The two larger men took up the stretcher. The largest, Gunnar, gave Odin a friendly smile. The girl thanked him once more.

Then, as shadowy as when they entered, they went out to the front porch, whispered to each other, and vanished into the night.

Jack Odin cleaned up the room and had another try at his letter. It was no use. An olive-skinned girl kept peering at him from the page. Her dark eyes laughing and filled with wonder, her dark curls sparkling with a few drops of mist—

He was sitting there an hour later, with scarcely a line written, when the next interruption came.

Heavy feet were upon the front porch. There was a loud knocking at the door.

He opened it again. Six men were there: an Army officer, two highway patrolmen, and three men in street clothes who showed their badges.

"Your name, sir?" asked the officer.

"None of your damned business," Odin told him, for it was late and he didn't like the man's face or tone.

"Your name!" It was an order.

"Doctor Jack Odin," the doctor shrugged. "Now, what's this all about?"

"Arrest, sir. Doctor Odin, you are under arrest for aiding and harboring the murderer of our Chief of Staff."

CHAPTER TWO

IT WAS two months before Doctor Jack Odin returned to his home. Christmas was nearing and the Star of the East was already shining in the sky as he got out of his car and looked up at the big, shadowy house. He shivered. Since men had first gone a-wandering, when had there been a more miserable homecoming?

Piles of leaves lay upon the walks. They complained beneath his feet as he stepped upon the porch.

Finding a key he opened the front door, turned on the light, and went in. Without thinking he locked the door behind him and dropped the key into his pocket. He shivered again. Two months ago—or two ages ago, depending on how you counted time—there had been another key, a larger key of ivory given to him by a breath-taking girl with golden eyes. Or had he dreamed of such a girl? Upstairs, in his bedroom, was the key. The only evidence of his sanity. The girl had not come forward. No one had ever admitted seeing her or the dwarfs. Many had sworn to the reality of the dark, wounded man—the dead General's secretary, the taxi-driver, and a tramp who had been on the Baltimore Road that night. The tramp had seen a car with the dark man slumped at the wheel. It had pulled slowly off the road and had headed toward Odin's house. But the man had never sworn positively that there was anyone else in the car. "I think there was—a smaller person—maybe a woman maybe some other people—"

Even the Forgans had to admit under oath that they had heard nor seen no one on that unlucky night.

A few days before his release, Odin had sent word to his

banker to have the house cleaned. Someone had done the job well, but the smell of years and dust, of old treasured things that had outlived their day and their masters, still clung to the rooms.

For a moment he wished that the Forgans were here. But he had arranged a pension for them, and they were now in Phoenix where Pete Forgan's rheumatism was doing better. So there was nothing left to do but walk alone.

The house-cleaner had stacked a few old newspapers upon an end table. After lighting the floor furnace, Odin sat down and looked at the headlines. Like trying to re-live a nightmare, he thought wryly.

His name was everywhere upon the front page. "ODIN ACQUITTAL PREDICTED," was the glaring headline. And near the center of the page the editor had prepared an editorial:

Doctor Mudd

Have we advanced since 1865? Will there be another Doctor Mudd? Mudd, as most readers know, was the innocent doctor who patched up Wilkes Booth. Because he performed a duty to an injured man, as any faithful doctor would do, Doctor Mudd was hauled off to Washington, given a mock trial and sentenced to Shark Island during that period of insanity that immediately followed the death of Lincoln. Now, another doctor is hauled off to Washington to stand trial before a Federal judge. Let us hope that we have advanced. There is nothing to link Doctor Odin with the death of General Mathew. The murderer was traced to Odin's house. There he was treated and disappeared. He has not since been seen. Odin tells a strange, almost unbelievable tale. No one has seen his golden girl or the dwarfs. If Odin is shielding a beautiful girl, as his accusers say, they should make every effort to find her. They should also find the murderer, whether he be a madman, anarchist, or Red. Let us have no more of this idiotic show, where a little-known doctor with an excellent war record is being made the scapegoat. No! We have had enough. Doctor Mudd will go free.

With a sigh Jack Odin let the paper drop to the floor. That editor had been friendly enough. Still, Odin had a feeling that his defenders had nearly ruined him. Things had taken a turn in those past months, which had placed him in a glaring light. He was either guilty or else he was the world's prize chump. Well, the editor had predicted correctly. He had been freed. The chump had been exonerated and proved to be a first-class chump indeed.

"Oh, hell," said Jack Odin. He got to his feet and began pacing about the room. Disgraced, embittered, and lonely. Good heavens, what could a pair of golden eyes do for a man. Eight years of study and four years of faithful service to the Air Force—faithful, maybe, certainly not excellent as the editor had insisted—all had gone down the drain. Golden eyes. Golden girl. Bah! He kicked the fallen paper into the farthest corner of the room.

Then there were steps upon the porch and voices. The voices he had heard once before. The strange language which was both alien and familiar. The same voices. He counted them. One, two, three, four. The fourth was a woman's. Low and musical, with just a breath of fear hovering over the syllables.

The footsteps and the voices stopped. There was a low, insistent rapping at the door.

He knew who was there. His first impulse was to dash out on the porch and kick all four of them into the yard. Then he discovered that he was as excited as a schoolboy, and was suddenly glad that the girl and her three dwarfs had returned. As he went to the door he cursed himself for a fool.

"Of all the idiots, Odin, you win the prize. Jail bait and trouble, that's all she is—"

But he opened the door and tried to appear as unconcerned as possible.

Maya was standing there, as straight and calm as before. Just as pretty too. She was bareheaded, though it was a cold night. A long red cloak was about her shoulders and pinned tightly at the throat. He bowed mockingly.

"Well, my friends. The battle is over, so you're here for your combat ribbons, no doubt."

She gave him a searching glance. The smile that had begun on bee-kissed lips faded away. She stepped into the room with a queenly air. The three dwarfs followed, looking much the same as they had before except that dark, woolen capes were thrown over their shoulders and the oldest, Jul, was wearing a red toboggan with a fluffy tassel that bobbed about as he walked. The other two, Gunnar and White Owl, saluted him quietly.

Still in a bad humor, Jack Odin closed the door and rubbed his hands together. "Well, well," he said, trying to be as sardonic as possible. "Here we are. Where have you been, may I ask, and what did you do with our patient—the murdering scum? You know, I'm not proud of that night's work."

"Please, Doctor." She acted as though she were getting ready to apologize and did not quite know what to say.

"Forget the 'doctor'," he said coldly. "Some gentlemen in Baltimore are deliberating this week as to whether or not I am worthy of that title—"

She did stamp her foot this time. "Oh," she sputtered, biting her lower lip in vexation, "Why are you so bothered? Oh—how do you say it—Fiddlesticks."

That made him madder than ever. "Fiddlesticks, is it? After what I've been through I ought to punch these little guys in the nose and take you across my knee and paddle the living daylights out of you."

She laughed. "I doubt if Gunnar would let you. I have known him to fell a bull with one blow of his fist."

This time, apparently, it was Gunnar's time to tell her to be quiet. He had been looking at Odin with a gleam of sympathy on his broad face.

The strong man's quiet dignity prompted Odin to set a better example.

"Well, there's no need of us standing here arguing. Sit down, all of you. I'm sorry I can't offer any refreshments. I just arrived, myself. In fact, I haven't been out of jail very long."

She removed a scarab clasp from her cape and threw the garment aside. Then she sat down in his favorite chair and smiled up at him. He noticed that instead of the sandals she now wore galoshes of red leather that were topped at the ankle by an inch of white fur.

"I'm sorry," she said. Then she laughed. It was a tinkly laugh, good-humored and honest. At the same time it irritated him.

"What's so funny?" Odin demanded.

"I am continually amazed at your race," she answered. There was a little smile of contempt hovering over her lips. "For nearly three months I have dodged in and out of your clumsy world and it is not to my liking. The people." A beautiful shoulder nearly touched the brushing dark curls as she shrugged. "They are impossible. Why do all of you try to be alike? Is it—what you call a propaganda medium instilled in you? Or is it nature's way of finally creating a host of dull, uninteresting people from the same mold. Now, Jack Odin, in our own, thoughtless way we have put you on what you call a spot. But I do not see that we have done such a terrible thing. You have offended the common thinking. Bah! Everywhere, I see people grimly pursuing what they call security. They do not appear exceedingly happy—and most of them are burdened down with what you call debts. Ugh."

The "ugh" made him boil again. "My race?" he questioned. "Dodging in and out of my world! Perhaps you have disowned us all, Milady?"

She smiled again and looked down at her red shoes. "Now, I have hurt your feelings again. But it is not my world and it is certainly not my race. For twenty-five thousand years and more the Brons have not taken the slightest interest in any of you."

"Your complex is showing now, eh? Well, what is wrong with our tendency to conform? Would you have a bunch of murderers sneaking around in the night? Stabbing people and getting stabbed? Then asking a bystander to patch you up so you can run away? By—uh, thunder—you're talking like we are a host of microbes creeping along on the withered skin of a half-rotten apple."

Her eyes met his, wavered and she looked down at her red shoes again. "I am sorry. I have offended you. In my land people do as they please as long as they don't annoy anyone. If they annoy another they soon get hurt. But if a man decides to go out and choke a tiger to death with his bare hands, we let him go. It may be a foolish thing to try, but it is his own affair."

"And where is this wonderful world of yours? You don't make it sound very inviting—" Odin remarked.

"I was using an extreme example. It would take a long time to explain my world to you. Anyway we are here to take you there."

"Me! Such crust! Now, where is the freedom you were talking about? Perhaps I don't give a whoop about seeing your world?" But Odin knew he was only blustering. Seeing any world with this exotic girl of the golden eyes appeared to be an excellent idea.

As though she sensed his thoughts, she drew her head up sharply and flung a dark curl away from her forehead.

"We have come because we owe you a debt. We have made things impossible for you in what appears to be an impossible world."

"Well," Odin admitted, "it isn't exactly a world of my own making. But I've grown up a bit in the last two months. Which probably means that I'm less gullible and less admirable. Now, tell me, did you come here to help me—or is there some other reason?"

Maya was even quite pretty when she frowned. "You are making things difficult. And you are getting ready to misunderstand. But there is also the key."

He laughed. "Now, we are uncovering the truth—"

With a little bound Maya was on her feet, golden eyes blazing. "You do not know how you were honored when we gave you that key. The key is a symbol of our lives. It belongs in our world. It and its owner. But you and the key can stay here—if that is the way you wish it. Jul, Gunnar, let us go."

So far, the dwarfs had kept still. Now, Gunnar came across the room. His swinging gait made him appear even shorter. His shoulders, so much wider than Odin's, were frightening.

Gunnar smiled. "This man has done some fighting in his day. You have talked to him like he was a carl." He held out a broad hand. "What we do is in the skeins of the Spinners. But you were welcome to go with us, soldier. Right welcome. As for the key, it is of little value. It has become—a symbol—but also, it has not been used. I am sorry for my part in that night's work—and I wish you well." With that he thrust his hand into Odin's.

Jack Odin took the proffered hand—and gripped back so hard that a grin of respect came to the dwarf's broad face. Odin laughed. "Now, there's an invitation I can accept. We'll look at this world of yours. And I'll take the key along. Lord, there are plenty of doors that need opening. And there are too many locks without any keys."

"Then you will go?" Maya asked archly, and Odin found himself fancying that she had not only wanted him to go, but had counted on his going all along.

"All the way," Jack told her, and laughed again as he quoted: "Up the Airy mountain, down the rushy glen—"

Maya and the dwarfs looked at each other in puzzled fashion. Then Old Jul spoke. "I think this is a man worthy of his name. He fashions him a farewell song. Eh, lad, were you ever a minnesinger?"

"Faith, no, old man, all the minnesingers are dead. My age had no use for them. You may have noticed that ours is one of those dreary stretches in time that is dedicated to only two things: The mediocre average and a sort of scientific barbarism."

Jul's back was bent and his white locks fell across his thin shoulders. But there was something about his face and his lofty brow that bespoke much learning and much thinking. His face, which was as pale and translucent as fine china, was seamed in thought. Then Jul asked: "I have heard that they crucified those they did not like. Were the minnesingers crucified?"

Odin was in a bitter mood. "And would they waste good oak? No old man, they laughed them off the stage and starved 'em to death."

Maya's lips began to pout at the delay. "Are you going to stay here while the night wastes away? Surely, you two don't have time to number the ills of this miserable land?"

"Or its good points, either." Jack flung himself to the rescue.

Again, the shiny, dark curls tossed commandingly. "It has no good points. If you are going, Jack Odin, I suggest that we be on our way."

A few minutes later, when Odin came down the stairs with the ivory and ruby key in one hand and a small overnight kit under his arm, they were growing impatient.

He looked about him. The old house was calling to him. All the things that were his and his mother's and father's before him were clamoring against being forsaken. He looked about him, trying to choose some souvenir to take along, but there were so many things that were dear to him.

Seeing his thoughts, Old Jul counseled, "There are but three things that a man can bring with him from the past: A dream, a memory, and a brave heart."

So Jack Odin let his companions out upon the porch and took one last look about him. It was one of those breathless, brutal moments when the hands of the clock swing down like flashing knives and sever the past from a man, so that he can say from then on: "Here, for good or bad, one chapter of my life ended and a new chapter began."

With a steady hand he turned out the light. Then he turned the knob and stepped out on the porch and closed the door softly behind him. The four were waiting in the yard. Above them the stars looked down with friendly eyes, winking occasionally to cheer them on.

Maya was driving. It was nearly midnight. Some sort of homing instinct seemed to guide her. Jack hadn't the slightest idea where they were. They had headed south, then west, then south again. Since the trial he had been bothered by headaches, and now one was coming on. It throbbed at his right temple until at last he groaned in pain. He was sitting between Jul and White Owl who had not spoken a word. Maya and Gunnar were in the front seat of the car, which was a cheap sedan about four years old, he judged.

"Tired?" Old Jul asked quietly.

"Yes, and a damnable headache too."

"Here." In the dark Odin could feel the old man's frail fingers feeling across the nape of his neck. They fluttered and kneaded, just as they had felt their way across the neck of the injured man that night when Odin had risked his diploma. It was a soothing, calming feeling. Not only were the nerves quieted, but Odin felt a sense of strength and well-being flooding through him as though the old man's small, knobby fingers were a connection to the vast surge of power leashed down deep in the earth. Just as he went to sleep, Odin had an odd feeling that he was a part of everything—the rocks and the trees, the birds and the birdsong, the teeming earth and the barren desert—living things and groping things—and he wondered how men could fight and wish each other ill when they were no more than sparks in that great flaming fountain which was leaping up into the dark sky in the distance. The fountain flamed higher, drew closer until he was in the very core of it, a spark flashing and swirling joyously with billions of other sparks—

And he slept.

It was high noon when he awoke. He was all alone in the back seat of the car that was parked in a thicket of scrubby oaks that still held to their dead leaves. The leaves were rattling against the barest trace of a wind. The sky was blue and the sunshine was warm, coming through the rolled-up windows. He looked about him. The leaves and the brown grass showed clearly that it was the same season of the year, but he must have traveled far to the southwest since leaving home.

He got out of the car, feeling strangely elated. No more despair or dejection was left. He was stronger. All the worries and the fear of disgrace that had plagued him were gone. Remembering a wild dream of a fountain of sparks rushing up the sky, those old troubles seemed trivial.

Then Odin heard a clang of steel against steel, and walking around a little knoll he saw Maya and the dwarfs active at something.

A cylinder of steel, about ten feet in diameter had recently thrust itself up through the reddish earth, so that it lay like the crest of a volcano at the top of a pyramid of rocks and clay. The four were busily shoveling earth away from it.

"Good morning," he called cheerfully as he walked toward them.

Maya put down her shovel and came to meet him. "Awake at last." She smiled. "My, they must have had you beat. I didn't realize you were so far gone. Do you know how long you slept, Dr. Odin?"

"Well, it's morning. About twelve hours," he guessed.

"And another morning. You slept for thirty-six hours, Jack Odin, while we drove to this place and worked after we got here."

He whistled his unbelief. "And what are you doing here? And what is that odd contraption you're digging up?"

"We're not digging it up. It has lain here at the center of a little hillock for ages—"

"Nonsense. It isn't rusty."

"You don't believe anything, Jack Odin. Now, I will tell you the truth. This is something like what you call an elevator. It goes far down into the earth—to the land of Opal where my people and the dwarfs have lived these thousands of years. Long ago my people used it for making expeditions to the face of the earth—but the trips were wearisome and unprofitable. It was abandoned, and the ages piled this heap upon the shaft. Only a few hours ago, we called for it and it thrust its way up. As soon as we clear the debris away and reach the door, we will be ready for our journey."

"Called it? Maya, you use some of the oddest expressions."

Maya stamped her foot. "Now, you are being stupid. We have a black box to control the machinery from miles away. Just as you can direct a rocket."

"Oh, I see. Wait a minute! You just said this thing was ages old. No machinery would last—"

It was her time to be scornful. "Nonsense. Our ancestors made machinery to last. Of course, we have used the machines so little. We found we had small need for them. Until lately—"

"Maya, here's the door," Gunnar called out. Jack Odin and the girl walked over to the excavation. The three dwarfs, even old Jul, were working furiously, throwing big shovels full of earth and gravel behind them. Jack marveled at their strength.

Soon an open shaft was made in the conical pile of debris about the base of the steel cone.

"It's clear, now," Gunnar cried out. The three came out of the shaft like gnomes.

Maya took up a small box that reminded Odin of an old-fashioned radio and started dialing.

There was a ghost of a squeak of metal against metal, and a convex door swung open in the side of the cylinder.

White Owl appeared to be the demolition squad for the group. He immediately got busy with some sticks of dynamite, buried them in the sides of the shaft and made some long fuses ready.

Gunnar was sweating. "Now, let's get out of here. I don't like it, Maya, never did. The whole trip has been a wild goose-chase, and we have found but one man to our liking."

"We—or Maya?" asked White Owl solemnly and winked at Jack.

"Indeed, we will go," Maya answered haughtily. "Someone may find a car they can use. Set the fuses, White Owl."

They crowded into the elevator. Control panels filled the circular sides of the little room. Odin looked about him in wonder.

Meanwhile, White Owl had lit the fuses and came scrambling into the elevator. Maya and Gunnar busied themselves with the controls. The door swung shut. Then the steel cylinder in which they were now sealed plummeted downward so swiftly that Odin nearly lost his breath. Above them came the muffled roar of the explosion that sealed the shaft once more.

The journey downward had begun.

CHAPTER THREE

GUNNAR took some folding chairs from a compartment behind one of the panels and set them up for his companions. After that, White Owl and Jul nodded like commuters.

One feeble bulb illuminated the elevator. Gunnar kept sitting down and getting up again to inspect the dials. Now and then the downward trip was halted or slowed while he and Maya set pressure regulators and oxygen gauges.

Once the light flickered strangely and Odin found himself wondering what would happen if their power was suddenly lost. Would they stop down here in the earth? Or would they go on down the shaft like a plummet? And how far had they gone? How deep down in the earth was this world that belonged to Maya and the dwarfs? He never got an answer to his questions. His friends dismissed them as of no importance. At one time he felt sure they were sliding downward at a forty-five degree angle, then the cylinder righted itself again and their descent was straight.

Finally Gunnar and Maya agreed that all was going well. While the heavy-shouldered little man sat with his eyes glued to the controls, Maya sat down by Jack Odin and brushed a moist curl from her forehead.

"Well, so far, Jack Odin. At least, you will start out in our world with a good name. Odin was a great hero to the dwarfs' ancestors. How did you come by that name?"

He shrugged. "How do we come by our names? Who can unriddle the past? You haven't answered the present riddle yet? In my time I've done some foolish things for some beautiful girls, but this is the first time I ever gave up everything I had and followed a beautiful one into a steel cage which apparently is falling to the center of the earth."

Maya smiled. "Were those other beautiful girls as pretty as this one?" she asked carelessly.

"Well—no," he answered.

She sighed. "It is a mixed-up affair, isn't it? You deserve to hear the story, but I will try to make it as short as possible. To give you the entire history of the Brons and the Neeblings would take weeks. And, as you just said, who can unriddle the past? So Jack Odin, be as patient and quiet as possible and I will tell you of the Brons and the Neeblings and their world of Opal."

Once, long ago, (Maya began) there was another sun with other planets. The sun began to misbehave. It flamed out, and the innermost planet melted in fervid heat. Then the sun drew back, but it was unsteady after that, and the other planets were becoming unbearable.

This was the solar system of the Brons, for my people owned all the planets. They had been going from world to world for centuries, but they had not dared outer space between the suns. Nor, I suppose, did they care to. But now it became necessary that they design a new ship, if even a remnant should survive. Their sun had become unstable, and perhaps at the next pulsation it would flame out into one vast nova and cinder all life that belonged to it—even the farthermost, ice-bound hulk of a planet which was almost lost on the fringe of space.

So new ships were prepared. Ships far different than the rocket things your troubled race is dreaming about. How many ships, I do not know, but the tale tells that there was a great number. A swarm, each stored with power enough to explore a galaxy. Swift and self-supporting, these ships.

I can only tell you of what happened to one. One ship, at least, escaped that threatening doom and plunged out into the void between the suns. From far away it watched its own sun melt and run down the sky.

In the one ship were ten couples. And at last it reached this planet of yours. But not the score who started the journey. Their children or grandchildren, for they had kept the same number aboard. This happened twenty-five thousand years ago.

They found your world forbidding, but it did support life similar to their own. The continents were different then, and the living things were somewhat different. They explored your world from pole to pole, but they found nothing but savages. Think of it, Jack Odin, in that far-off day your people might have been taught to bridge the gap between the hunting-fire and atom-heat. But they would have nothing of the Brons. Wherever my people went they were attacked by yelling savages, who were slaughtered in droves, but who kept coming back.

The Brons were considering a plan to make a part of the moon over into a grim but inhabitable land when they discovered the Neeblings. These people, as you may have guessed, are of Norse stock. They alone had flocks and smiths. But they were hated as much as the Brons. I think they were on the verge of extermination when they met us. The races of men have always hated anything that was different. And, as you can see, they are different from other men. Though they grazed their flocks in the pastures above ground they lived in caves by night. They, I am sure, are the Trolls and the Little People who Live Under the Hills who have survived in your legends to this day. They knew the caves and the tunnels underground, the Neeblings. They had found a vast, dark hollow in the earth, far, far below. Though it was dark and forbidding, they had dreamed of living there away from their enemies. An impossible dream, at that time, but with the coming of the Brons it became reality. That forbidding bubble of blackness that they found finally became our beautiful world of Opal. We think it is the shell that was left when some moonlet hardened like a seed and was hurled forth into space just before the bubbling earth cooled into shape. At any rate, we and the Neeblings bought that world and paid for it with nine generations of lives. It seems to be a law of the universe, Jack Odin, that nothing can be gained without full payment.

Opal, as you will soon discover, is an elliptical disc with sheer sides and an out-curved ceiling. Our ancestors dismantled their ship and moved it. Of their atomic power, they and the Neeblings built a tiny, artificial sun at the highest point of the ceiling, five miles above ground. They opened a passageway to the sea and let in water until all the land that was left was several peninsulas thrust out from the base of the cliffs. They brought in plants, insects, birds and animals—all that they could find, rejecting none, lest they lose some balance of nature. With the coming of the seawater came the living things of the sea. Then they closed that passageway, leaving a great door so they could have an escape route if it were needed.

Some of the things they brought there soon died. Others lived or changed to adjust themselves. So the land of Opal was built and paid for with the lives of the Brons and the Neeblings. And there we have lived all these centuries, not bothering the upper world except to listen in upon your quarrels and idiocies occasionally. Not bothered by you until of late.

Maya finished her story. She sighed and got up to help Gunnar with some of the controls. They were now sliding down an incline at a furious rate. Their momentum slowed. The capsule of steel eventually righted itself and, still slowing, resumed its vertical position once more.

Assured that Gunnar needed no more help, the girl came back to her chair.

"And that is our story, Jack Odin," she said quietly.

He had not interrupted. But already a throng of questions clamored for an answer. Assuming that Maya's story was true, and not a mere jumble of myths, what vistas into the past were opened? Then, suddenly, he realized that he had been swindled again. He had wanted to know the reason for the death of a respected general; instead, he had received a mere saga, which purportedly came within twenty-five thousand years of the present.

"And is it?" he retorted scornfully. "Is it, indeed? It sounds more like moonshine. But where does it concern us? Why have you been skulking around up there like a passel of whipped dogs? Why was General Mathew killed? And what became of this devil who I patched up?"

Golden eyes flashed. Maya's chin held high, she blazed at him: "We do not skulk. Nor are we whipped dogs. Oh, we had hopes for you once. But when Atlantis went beneath the waves, there was nothing left but barbarians beating themselves over the heads with stone clubs. Only the hard-headed survived—as any fool can plainly see."

"So I made you mad, did I? Well, I'm plenty mad myself. It seems to me like you're one of those unfortunate individuals who have been educated from an over-edited history book. Now, tell me the truth about the swine who caused me all that trouble before I lose my temper and shake the spit out of you."

Maya was still blazing. "Gunnar would break you in two for that remark."

"He's got good shoulders and arms, I'll admit. But I've taken some who were taller. Besides, he looks to me like a guy who wouldn't fight without a sound reason. Oh, hell, I don't want to fight Gunnar. But you're as exasperating a female as I ever tangled with."

"Now, Doctor," she mocked. "Don't diagnose a case until you have spent at least a thousand dollars on clinical tests. You may, if I understand your profession, be able to give me a pill. A pill to wake a person up and a pill to put him asleep again. Good heavens, what a way to make a living!"

"It's an old and honorable profession. And now I am burned up. I am not a doctor any more. And you know why. Because I patched up that murdering scum you brought to my house. Such crust! And I suppose the people of your country cure themselves with dirt dauber's nests and vinegar. Or do they hire witch doctors?"

"They don't get sick," she answered simply.

"Okay. Okay. Now, for the last time, will you tell me why you were wandering around the District and who was that character I patched up?"

Her eyes were no longer flashing. Maya appeared to be a bit ashamed of her remarks as she started up to help Gunnar.

Odin clutched her arm. "He needs no help— Now, the truth—"

Maya shook her arm free. Then, staring straight ahead, she answered, "His name is Grim Hagen. He is my cousin."

"Every family has at least one, I suppose."

"I do not like Grim Hagen. I am not excusing him. But in the world of Opal he is one of the highest-ranking five."

"He is! They must select them by playing bingo. And who are the others?"

"Jul is one," Maya answered. "I am another—"

Odin bowed. "Excuse me for what I just said, princess."

"You are laughing again. The fourth is the chief of the scientists."

"So these are your best, eh?" Odin felt like being scornful, for she had said too much against his world and his profession. "A girl, a murdering louse, a little old man, and a scientist who probably brews bat wing stew. Who's the fifth?"

Maya lifted one foot and studied it carefully.

"Who's the fifth?"

Maya flashed him a breathtaking smile and said: "You are."

"Me? Will you please be serious."

"I am," Maya protested. "The keys govern. There are five. Grim Hagen and I each heired one from our fathers. Jul, the patriarch of the Neeblings, has one according to a very old law. The chief scientist has another, but the scientists refuse to have anything to do with selecting the fifth. The owner of the fifth key is to be selected by three.

He must be a good, honorable man, likely to put the general welfare above his own wishes. The holder of the fifth key had died shortly before we made the trip to your land. We kept his key with us, as the law required. Then, that night, with Grim Hagen not voting, Jul and I gave it to you. I told you it was a great honor—"

"Now, I'll try to be humble and thank you. But why?" asked Odin.

"It seemed to us that one of your race should sit in our councils. Things had got out of hand. Whether you liked it or not, your race had got too involved in our affairs. And we liked you better than any we had met."

"I am honored," Odin told her quietly, "but you must have met very few. And it is still a riddle to me."

"Our artificial sun," Maya explained, "is a regulated atomic fire. Different from your atom blasts, different from your isotopes. As benevolent as your own sun. So it would have stayed had you not begun your atomic blasts. With your first blast, it flickered. It has continued to flicker and wink out with every blast. Sometimes, a mere wink. At other times it has left us in pitch-dark for hours. It is not a mere burning of uranium particles. We are far below the earth's surface, but some of our energy comes from the sun itself. Out there in the depths of space my ancestors used the energy of the suns. Your atomic explosions come through, making something similar to what you call a short-circuit. Without our sun we would grope in the dark for a few weeks. Then we would die. Assuming that the last explosion that burned out our sun did not poison us with its rays."

"And you think I can help? Maya, my country is no longer the only one with atom bombs."

"I know. But Jul liked you—and I—well, I liked you too. Grim Hagen was violent when he recovered, but we do not take orders from Grim Hagen. Not yet. You see, our visit to

Washington was to arrange a secret meeting with the Chief of Staff. Grim Hagen thought he could persuade the general, but as usual Grim lost his temper."

"But why didn't you go to the President?"

"Grim Hagen thought it best to see the Chief of Staff. Oh, I don't know what was in Grim's mind. Jul and I let him persuade us."

Suddenly the deceleration of the elevator was breath taking, weighting them down. Then Gunnar brought the steel cylinder to a stop with one last swoop that made Odin bob in his chair. Gunnar looked over his shoulder with a smile on his broad face. "Home again," he announced, and pulled a lever.

The elevator door opened and another one opened beyond.

To Jack Odin it was like seeing a framed picture of fairyland. Their door had opened in the face of a cliff, fully three hundred feet above the world below. A stairway of gold-flecked marble led downward to a plain. In the distance was a city with lofty spires and minarets. It glimmered beneath a tiny sun that was set into the very center of a turquoise bowl of sky. Glimmered was the word, for these towers seemed to be fashioned of rose marble and new ivory, of silver and gold, with here and there the very palest of robin's egg blue to add a breath of coolness. Beneath the city, and on the plain before and beyond, the gardens and forests were like emerald waves. The trees were mostly palm and giant fern, Jack Odin guessed, but the undergrowth must have been at least six feet high. Off in the distance was a sea, and above the opalescent water were billowing white clouds. The sea was motionless. The sky merged into a misty silver in the distance. The horizon was indistinct.

There was no welcoming party. The five walked out upon

the steps. The air was warm and fresh and clean. Far below, songbirds were singing a chorus. Then Gunnar closed the two doors and they walked down to the plain. As they descended, Jack Odin saw a tiny white road that came out of the city and through the underbrush to meet them. He guessed that it was made of crushed shell, for it too glimmered in the sun.

They came to the road. Jack offered Maya his arm but she shook it away. She walked with a lithe, swinging gait, and the dwarfs, for all their short legs, kept up a trotting pace that made Odin step along.

Suddenly he had a feeling that something was following them. Once he was sure that he saw a shadow, halfway up the bole of a palm. And once he was sure he saw two eyes peering at him from a heavy clump of bushes. But there was a constant scurrying of feet, claws, and feelers out there. The birds and the tree toads were clamoring. Grasshoppers and katydids were at their old symphonies. He could not be sure that he heard any sound that could be separated from the steady drone, though he noticed that Gunnar watched the same side of the road.

Then, without warning, the sun flickered once and went out.

They were in stygian dark for a moment. The birds and the insects had stopped their song. But off to one side, near the spot that Gunnar and Odin had been watching, came a horrible screaming.

Maya turned on her pocket torch and held it high. And just at that moment an ape-like thing came shuffling out of the dark. It screamed again as it rushed toward them.

With a war cry of a Viking Gunnar turned aside to meet it, his long arms outspread.

They met. The thing was neither chimp, nor gorilla, nor orangutan, but somewhere in between. It kept on yammering as it advanced. The girl moved forward, holding her electric torch high, trying to blind it.

With a rush it was upon Gunnar. Ape-like hands clutched the dwarf's throat, and Gunnar embraced the thing. His long arms went under the brute's armpits. His hands came up and forward, locking themselves about that slanting forehead. For a moment they stood there, weaving, Gunnar holding the creature's teeth only a few inches from his throat. Then they slipped and fell.

"Here," Jul thrust the handle of a knife into Odin's hands. "Get him, Nors-king."

Without thinking of the title that had been thrust upon him, Odin leaped forward. The thing had fallen across Gunnar though the dwarf was still holding its head away from his throat and slowly bending its neck back. Odin started to stab at the ribs, but the ape was struggling so violently that he feared he would hurt Gunnar. The thing had a fringe of coarse hair that ran from crown to nape. This he seized with one hand, and with Gunnar helping to hold the brute, Odin slashed its throat as neatly as any hog-killer.

Gunnar rolled clear of the fallen body and wiped its blood from his face.

"Eh," he said, and laughed a wild laugh. "So Odin comes back to the roots of Yggdrasil where time and men and life and space began. Now let the Norns take up the skeins. For at last we have a man on our side. And Nidhoggr the dragon shall tremble. Let the thunder roar and the lightning flash, for the anvil will shiver beneath the hammer. And the smith will leave nothing but good clean steel at the forge."

Then as suddenly as it had left them, the little sun flickered and came back to warm life. The insects and the birds took up their song.

Gunnar looked down at his bloody hands, wiped them upon his thighs with a guttural laugh, and held out his hand to Odin.

Odin transferred the dripping knife to his left hand, and gripped Gunnar's with all his strength.

Then Gunnar laughed and clasped Odin about the arm with his free hand. "Blood brothers, now. And I will fight beside you. Like a storm. Like a flame—"

Maya switched off her electric torch and put it back into its holster at her belt.

Her eyes had first narrowed at Gunnar's outburst. But now they were open and determined. "See, Jack Odin. This was but a touch of what we sometimes get. Imagine twenty-four hours of this—in a city, or on the beaches where the things come up from the deep?"

Jack wiped his forehead. "This was bad enough. Do you let these creatures run wild so near the city?"

"And why not?" she questioned. "The hunters must have their kill."

He bowed mockingly. "Princess, what an outlook."

Odin cleaned the knife on a broad leaf and returned it to Jul. Then they took up their march to the city, which gleamed brighter and towered higher as they approached.

CHAPTER FOUR

AS THEY went down the shell-topped road that ran between verdant walls of foliage, Jack Odin had a feeling that he was walking toward the center of a great shallow bowl. That feeling never left him altogether. As Maya had told him, the world of Opal was disc-shaped with sheer walls and an out-curved roof. The shallow sea, almost wave-less, shimmered in the distance. The road, the jungle about it, and the town itself were a part of a peninsula that jutted out from the wall. Indeed, he learned later, most of the habitable land of Opal was made up of peninsulas such as this. There were a few scattered islands, but they were small and of little consequence.

He watched the sea as they descended. It was not completely tide-less, he judged, but it had a painted, glimmering look—like, well, like an opal. This world was rightly named. Strictly speaking, there was no horizon. Vision simply failed at a point where steam-banks were thickest. There were a few boats in the distance. They had neither sails, nor oars, nor funnels. No puffs of smoke were above them. Yet, they were moving—quietly, calmly. Far away was one tiny island little more than a shadow against the water, with one darkling cloud gathering above it. A few wedge-shaped flights of sea birds were piercing their way through the sky. He watched one flight until it reached the vanishing point. At no time did the formation waver or change.

Then the road leveled off and the city was before them, hiding the sea from view. This was Maya's city—Valla she had called it—and with its domes, minarets, and spires, all blue and ivory and rose, with here and there a flash of silver and gold, it looked like a faery city lost out of elfland. Birds filled the sky above it, weaving their old, familiar patterns into the summery day. Odin had forgotten how to cry, but there was a lump in his throat as he looked at the beauty spread out before him, as though something lost or something dreamed about long and long ago had suddenly reappeared. Two mocking birds were singing nearby, each one trying to build the brightest bubble of glittering notes upon the June day air.

There were no slums hanging to the outskirts of this city. Valla, Maya told him, had a population of not over forty thousand. But each house and tower was built within the center of a city block, with gardens and lawns and fences about it, so that Maya's city gave the appearance of being much larger than this.

Nor did their sudden appearance upon the sidewalks create any great interest. Even Odin's clothes did not attract much attention. A few children ran to the fences and called out to them. Odin heard the word "Maya" repeated often. The girl and the dwarfs answered the greetings, stopping occasionally to talk, and once White Owl left them to tell a joke to an old acquaintance, and came running to catch up, still laughing. He had been the glummest of the lot, Odin had thought, but now that he was home the little man was out of the doldrums.

Some dogs barked. A few strollers greeted them pleasantly, took a quick look at Odin and shrugged their shoulders. But the little party might as well have been returning from an afternoon's fishing trip for all the welcome that was given them.

Odin had started out carrying his coat across his arm, but on Maya's and Gunnar's advice he had thrown it away. Maya and the dwarfs had left their winter clothes in the elevator, and had put on lighter wear and sandals. Odin was becoming uncomfortably warm as they neared the center of the town. There were more and more people on the street, and Maya stopped to talk several times while Odin perspired and mopped his face with a wet handkerchief, feeling as out of place here as he ever had in his life.

Then they came to a three-storied house of rose marble, set behind a low wall of white stone. Maya opened a gate and they went into a yard that was shining with flowers and well kept shrubs. The gate closed behind them and she gave Odin a flashing smile.

"Well, this is home. We Brons like privacy, as you can tell. We respect it and we demand it."

They went across a columned porch that felt suddenly cool and restful. Then Maya let them into a large room that was so inviting and so filled with art treasures that Jack Odin stood dumbfounded. He whistled. "This room would cost a fortune in Washington."

She picked up a statuette of a golden girl. "This was given to me, but most of the things here were made by me or my people. Just as this house was built by my ancestors, block by block. We buy and sell very little—"

Gunnar, who seemed as much at home here as Maya, took Odin upstairs and gave him a room with a marble bath adjoining which was nearly as large as the room itself.

The water in the bath was slightly salty. Odin would have stayed there with his chin barely out of the water for an hour or two, but Gunnar hurried him out. The clothes that the little man brought him was something like linen, but even lighter. They were not greatly different from the summer clothes that Jack had left in Maryland. All were monogrammed with a red and ivory key—even the socks and shorts. The trousers were light gray and the loose-fitting shirt was a shade darker. Odin was to learn that the men of this world of Opal had a distaste for white—although they had nothing against flaming colors, even in silk or nylon. But, just as in the world above, he was never able to account for any particular fashion or style.

Much refreshed and cooler, Odin stood at the window and looked down at the fine yard below. The shadows lay like black stripes across the green lawn. He wondered what time it was. And then remembered that those shadows always stayed the same.

Gunnar brought a pair of sandals and a small gold chain.

"What's this?" Odin asked, looking at the tiny links with admiration.

"You had better put the key on it and wear it around your neck and under your shirt," Gunnar advised. "The key means much here. Maya tells some fine tales about her people, but men have died for that key before."

"It will make an awkward dog tag, friend."

"Eh, I do not understand. Oh, yes, you have been a soldier. Well, I have done some soldiering too—"

"And what would a land like this need with soldiers?"

Gunnar laughed. "Half our time is spent in fighting. There are the volps—the brute-things of the woods—you killed one of them for me. They eat both flesh and crops, even as men. Then, years ago, there were some who became pirates and lived on one of the islands. We left them alone, until they started raiding us. For a man should do as he pleases unless he harms other men. Then we wiped them out. Oh, it was a good fight. I have been bored ever since. But these things do not matter. It is the every-day fighting that matters. You see, Nors-King, my people are herdsmen and growers of crops. There are probably as many wild things in this smaller land than there are in the entire world above. We must fight—"

"But why don't you destroy them, as we did?"

"Are you any happier after destroying your wild things?" Gunnar asked simply. "Then too there is always the chance that a man will provoke you just for the sport of it."

"Good heavens! You make this world sound a great deal different than Maya's world. How about fair play? How about courts? This sounds like a school playground in a tough district when all the teachers are away."

Gunnar's eyes were both twinkling and sad. "At least we are honest about it. Should we set up some institution to protect us when it too might finally become a tyranny?"

"Another thing I don't understand, friend Gunnar, is how you manage to speak my language so well—and in such a short time—?"

"Oh, we have devices to hear through the miles of rock above us. We have taken recordings of your world from time to time. So, please, don't say you are better than we. Anyway, we learned a smattering of your language before we started on that ill-fated journey."

"I see. Now, excuse me for asking these questions. But I know so little about you—"

"That is one of the reasons I am here. Another reason is that I have liked you since we first met—and we have fought side by side."

"Then, if you are a herdsman and farmer, why are you here?"

"Maya sent for us—especially for Jul who was a friend of her father and his father before him. Jul is a very old man. As you probably have surmised, all is not too well with this world, Jack Odin."

"Yeah, it's ailing. Even as my own. But what can we do about it?"

Gunnar laughed. "You have just arrived, and now you are ready to cure all our woes. Within a short time our sun will begin to wane. I suggest that we eat supper."

"Okay. Okay. I'm squelched, and I'm hungry."

Maya's dining room was large enough for a score of people. The walls were covered with excellent paintings— mostly in reds and blacks. Although there was one scene of a beach with tired waves coming in and low dark clouds gathered above a lone boat wearily beating its way to shore.

Jul was seated at the head of the huge, hand-carved table—Maya to his right, Gunnar and Odin to his left. Below them was a wide expanse of linen tablecloth, with a centerpiece of crimson and orange flowers. These were some sort of tulips, Odin judged, but they were larger than any he had ever seen and had a peculiar, waxy sheen to them as though at any time they might melt and change their shape back to some pristine flower from which they had developed.

The silver and china were beautiful and old. The crystal was so thin that there was a whisper of notes from it at a touch. The food was good—not too different from the world above. There was a small fowl for each of them, cooked with wild rice in a rich sauce. There was a vegetable that tasted like asparagus, but was in the shape of a tiny green-white bulb. Maya's bread more like an English scone; these biscuits and a bowl of fruit completed the meal.

There were no servants in the house. Maya and Jul were talking in that strange but slightly familiar language which had puzzled Jack Odin from the first. Gunnar entertained him with a few more tales of Opal, reminding him that he had never lived until he had fought a cave bear. And then, abruptly, the dwarf asked:

"How are you with—what you call it—the lariat?"

Odin laughed. "Outside of one summer on a western ranch when I was a kid, I never used one. An old cowhand taught me a few tricks, but I'm afraid I forgot them long ago."

"Never mind. I will teach you again. Here, in Opal, you would not have forgotten such things. Sometimes I think that Grim Hagen is right. In your world you are so busy making a living that you forget all about living."

Jack borrowed some of Gunnar's own words. "You were up there for a very short time, my friend, and now you are ready to cure all our woes."

Gunnar laughed. "That was a good thrust. Anyway, I will teach you the—uh—lariat. Here we call it a thon, and our lariat is made of braided leather."

"The old cowhand told me that his first lariat was the same. And I'll be glad to learn—"

"And the sword? How can you handle it—"

"Well, I was a fencing champion once."

"Fencing champion?" Gunnar's brows knitted in thought.

Then he laughed again. "Oh, yes, I remember. Those tiny weapons, like long needles. The face and chest protected. Oh, well, you may have learned something. Here we use a heavier sword. I prefer the broadsword. It makes up for my lack of height." He looked up at Odin's shoulders, which were above the crown of the dwarf's head. One wistful look betrayed him. Then he was his usual self as he shrugged. "Oh, well, there is no man, tall or short, who can beat Gunnar."

"But why this business of swords and lariats?" Odin asked. "Maya said you had atomic power at hand. Failing that, you could use gunpowder. Or would that be sporting?"

Gunnar jerked a broad thumb toward the ceiling. "Up there is a man-made sun. Beyond it are billions of tons of stone. One does not take a chance when his sky might fall upon him. Even a motor that makes noise is outlawed. All of us hate noise. Still, there are some old tales that ten of us flying through the air with little humming motors strapped to our backs. Eh, Nors-King I can't answer all your questions. This is a very old land. Perhaps we have improved. Perhaps we have lost some of the things we once knew. I am a herdsman and sometimes a soldier. You will have to go to the Philosophers for the answers to your questions. Meanwhile, it is time for our sun to wane. I never fail to enjoy the sight. Odin, I envy you this first look at our world. It is a grand experience."

Gunnar moved out of his chair, excused himself to Maya and Jul and motioned for their guest to follow.

Out in the yard, Gunnar consulted an old-fashioned pocket watch that had twenty-four runes upon it and said:

"It will begin. Don't look up until I tell you."

There was a warning flicker of light—a pause—then two more flickers. Slowly the light faded from the lawn as though drawn swiftly upward. In another minute there was a ghostly twilight. In less than five, night had fallen. Odin looked up. The sun had dwined to the faintest ghost of a moon. Man-made stars were peeking out. Familiar patterns—the Dipper, especially—were twinkling up there. Like lights on a signboard, Jack Odin thought, for these stars seemed close enough to touch. And then a doubting question entered his mind. Why the Dipper? Those stars were certainly not shining through the shell of stone between this world and them. What would Maya's people have cared about the Dipper?

"For guiding the ships at sea?" Gunnar murmured, as he sensed Odin's questioning. In twelve more hours, our sun will wax once more and the stars will disappear. It is better to go in now."

Indeed it was. There was a noticeable chill in the air and already the dew was gathering on the grass.

They returned to Maya's large living room just as the girl and Jul appeared. Odin detected a faint whirr of machines coming from the direction of the dining room and the kitchen beyond. Evidently, housekeeping was not a great problem in this world of Maya's.

Odin was so interested in the art treasures about them that Maya took two from the wall and handed them to him. One was a mosaic about two feet square of a tiger creeping out from a jungle of mother-of-pearl and jade. The sky above was turquoise and aquamarine. The tiger was jet and topaz. Two magnificent cat's-eyes dominated the mosaic, and bloodstone and ivory made up the widening mouth of the on-rushing cat. Odin gasped. Aside from the artwork and the endless hours of labor that had gone into this piece, the stones and bits that made up the mosaic were worth a fortune.

"My grandmother made that," Maya told him proudly.

"The other is much older, a mirror—jetsam of Atlantis which one of our ancestors brought back from the floor of the sea. Is it not lovely?"

It was smaller than the mosaic. The polished surface of the mirror was as bright as though it had been fashioned yesterday. About it was a two-inch frame of gold, wondrously carved. Mermaids and nereids beckoned, tossed their flowing curls at Triton, or dodged an on-rushing sea-dragon mockingly. The entire frame of softest gold appeared to be alive with movement.

"This is one of Atlantis' lesser works," Maya said softly as Odin studied the carving in wonder. "They had a temple a mile square, where gold and silver and chryselephantine carvings never seemed to stop moving. Movement was in all their art. Not like the Egyptians where movement was frozen into art. Still, I have one Egyptian statuette that I may show you some day. An ivory girl with a body that would make your movie queens retire—an ivory girl with the head of a vulture. That head was carved from a single pigeon's blood ruby. It is said that Cheops gave a thousand slaves for this statuette. It and the golden mask were to be the central treasures of Tut-Ankh-Amen's tomb. But thieves stole it from him. An ancestor of mine took it from a soldier in Babylon who was about to break the head away from the body. He severed the soldier's head first—of course."

There was a sound of footsteps at the door. The chime of silver bells.

Maya opened the door. There stood Grim Hagen, Odin's sometime patient. He was dressed in scarlet and black. At his side hung a short scabbard with a gold handle of a sword gleaming from it. Tall and lean, he looked down at Maya and smiled sardonically. "What is this I hear of you bringing an ape from the upper world to trouble us?" He spoke these words in his own language, but later Maya interpreted them to Odin.

She started to slam the door, but he caught it with his shoulder and advanced. Behind him came two others, each as tall and lithe as Grim Hagen. These too were armed. A short sword hung from each belt and at the other side hung a coiled leather lariat.

The three came in and closed the door behind them. Jul, who had been seated in a large chair with his chin resting upon his hands, looked up at them in wonder.

"So you enter the house of a princess in such fashion, Grim Hagen?" he asked thoughtfully. "I am speaking in English. Answer in the same language lest we offend our guest."

"Be quiet, old man. Go back to your fields and pastures. It will soon be calving time."

"The creatures of the field suffer patiently and are little trouble. The good God keeps them going year by year. The panther kills and ravens. But in time the panther looks death in the face and does not find it good. I am of the Neeblings. Shall I foretell your fate, Grim Hagen?"

"My fate is lost among the stars. The stars my people lost so long ago. It is the present that is my concern. This upperape has been brought here. He has been given one of the keys. That is your work, Jul, yours and Maya's. I come for the key. If my cousin chooses to mate with an ape, that is her concern—"

That was enough for Odin. He stepped forward, fists swinging. For weeks now he had thought it would be so nice to get his hands on that tall, lithe man who had caused him so much trouble. But Grim Hagen stepped aside, and one of his lieutenants met Odin head-on.

They grappled. For a moment, Odin was reminded of the time when he, the greenest of freshmen, had stepped into the ring with an experienced man. This opponent was nearly forty pounds lighter than himself. Still, the man thrust Odin's arms up neatly, got a good grip at the small of his back, and started bending him. Odin lifted his hands up high and brought them down with all his strength.

His opponent lost his grip and stepped back. When he came in again, Odin swung an uppercut that lifted the fellow to his toes. The man went down like he was poured.

Odin turned about. He hadn't the slightest idea what the rules of the fight were. Korea had taught him that it was much better to play without any rules. Grim Hagen still stood arrogantly aside, his hand upon the hilt of his sword. But the remaining lieutenant had drawn his blade when he saw his comrade go down. He advanced, thrusting as he came. Then Gunnar stepped forward, swooping low, catching the soldier's wrist in his big hand. For a moment they stood there swaying, the soldier looking down into Gunnar's face, his teeth clenched, his eyes staring. They struggled. Then there was a snapping sound as of green wood breaking. The sword fell to the floor. Gunnar stepped back, and the soldier stood there with tears of pain in his eyes as he looked down at a wrist which had suddenly become V-shaped.

Now Grim Hagen had drawn his sword, but Gunnar stood his ground. Jack Odin took up a chair and advanced from the side.

"Not now," Gunnar laughed. "Later, Grim Hagen, when I can do the job much more slowly. Now, take your two men and go. But take one last look at the man who saved your life up there. The Aesir have taken up the skeins. I am not the seer that Jul is, but if I don't kill you, Grim Hagen, this man will—"

Grim Hagen's face was dark with wrath. "I will speak in the ape-thing's tongue, so he can understand. He and the

Neeblings have signed their death warrant tonight. And, Maya, who once I asked to be my bride, some day you shall be my slave. I promise that you shall see the end of this world as well as the world above. Sun after sun, planet after planet, these shall be mine. Our people hid like rats in a cave, while the galaxy was waiting to be picked like ripe fruit. Well, no more. The suns shall tremble and the worlds shall quake in fear. The moons shall run down the sky in streamers of light. The old outrage can never be paid. All the gold that could be heaped into this world would not pay it now. Always, there would be some ancient hurt and hate uncovered. I swear it now, the universe shall pay the price, with all the waiting and all the hating heaped upon the scales. It shall pay, and you shall see the smoke of worlds you have never seen. And all that while you shall be my slave—"

"Go, now," Jul said softly. "You have said too much already. Go now, before I let Gunnar kill you."

"I am not afraid of Gunnar, but I am going."

"Then go," Gunnar ordered, his feet braced wide apart.

Grim Hagen and the man with the broken wrist helped the fallen, groaning soldier to his feet. The three went staggering out the doorway, as beaten and sorry a crew as Odin had ever seen in his soldiering. But the hate that they left behind hung in the air in heavy waves.

Gunnar took the matter carelessly, even joking about the fight. Maya was troubled. Old Jul had a faraway look in his pale-blue eyes. And Odin fell to wondering what would happen if some day he and Grim Hagen met face to face and alone.

CHAPTER FIVE

DOCTOR Jack Odin and Gunnar were indulging in a bit of spirited swordplay and doing some definite damage to Maya's well-kept lawn.

Odin had fancied himself something of a fencer, but Gunnar was more than a match. He was built so low to the ground. He came forward, sidling like a crab, and he was so quick on his feet that there wasn't any way of knowing where he would next stand. The swords flashed and clanged together. Then Odin's blade was twisted from his hands and flew through the air to land in a choice flowerbed some twenty feet away.

Odin felt helpless and chagrined, but Gunnar thrust his straight blade into the ground and came forward to meet him with a whoop.

"Eh, you are doing better, Nors-King, much better. In time you will have me scrambling. Now for the thons. Remember, a small loop thrown by the wrist. It can be used as a whip too. But don't be off balance and let some carl grab it and draw you to him. Many a good lad has died that way."

Odin ignored the proffered rawhide lariat and sat down upon a cast-iron bench. "Later, friend Gunnar. Later. My shoulders are aching. And I have things on my mind. A few things to mull over—"

Gunnar sat beside him and mopped his forehead.

"Things to mull over, eh? And could those things be a woman?" He grinned. "Well, I have lost much time these past days. Waiting for Jul to decide what only the Norns can decide. Teaching you to improve yourself. Never have I seen a man whose education has been so neglected. What do those churls up above do with their bodies?"

"I have kept myself in pretty good shape," Jack Odin retorted.

Gunnar chuckled. "You felled Grim Hagen's man right neatly that night. But if you are one of the better specimens, how do the poorer creatures live? They must go in constant fear of death, being as weak as they are."

"Nobody would hurt them. At least, very few would. They get some exercise by going to work and dodging traffic when they cross the streets."

"The poor souls. Well, I must send a few things to the farm. My wife, Freida, will think I have gone a-voyaging. And I should write a letter. So you sit here and think, and Gunnar will go about his business."

"I didn't know you had a wife."

"Oh, yes, and seven children. Freida will look after the place, while I am gone. The Neebling women have always done so when their men take the wanderlust. They do not worry. Freida's arms are nearly as large as mine. You do not pick your women for strength, Jack Odin. Maybe that is why all of you have gone to seed."

"Nonsense. Our women like pretty clothes and perfume, but right now there are probably plenty of women looking after ranches larger than yours."

Gunnar was thinking again. "I see. You keep the better ones on the farms and ranches and send the skinny undesirables to the cities."

"Confound it, I didn't say that—"

"Oh well, I should write to mine Freida and order a load of hay. Don't think too hard, friend Odin. Thinking saps the strength and makes a man weak."

With a playful punch at Odin's shoulder, which almost numbed him, Gunnar went across the lawn, rolling as he walked on stout short legs, and disappeared down the street.

Odin sat there in the warm sunlight, his eyes half-closed, thinking of the two weeks that had passed, of the fight in Maya's house, of Gunnar, of Maya's golden eyes and her smooth tan skin. Of the things he had learned and seen, the art treasures, the beautiful days in this land where it was always June, of Maya's golden eyes and her pouting lips, of the society here below, the few customs he had learned, the people he had met.

He opened his eyes and sat up straight. This was no time for daydreaming. Pull yourself together, he advised himself. No more wool gathering. Think. Remember. Sort out everything you have learned. Time's running out, and you had better learn as much as you can, Jack Odin, or you're a dead pigeon.

It was hard to think in such a land as this. A six-inch butterfly, all purple and gold, went sailing across the lawn. Mocking birds were singing. The perfume of flowers and the grass under his feet, the smell of growing things, all these made the air heavy with sleep, and sparkling with an old wonder that the air up above had lost.

Daily, for the past fourteen days, he and Gunnar had worked with the sword and the thon. In addition to the clothes that had been given him upon his arrival in Opal, Jack Odin now owned a scabbard and blade, a wide belt, a leather lariat, and a watch.

The language had come easy. On the second day, despairing of ever learning it, Odin had taken pen and paper and had written down a few words phonetically. It was Old Norse, unmistakably, so kin to Anglo Saxon that he had once studied that Gunnar was able to understand the few sentences of Beowulf that Odin recited. After that, the lessons went faster. Also, Maya had set aside two hours of each day for her teaching, and with such an instructor a man had to apply himself if he didn't look too long into a pair of golden eyes.

The swordsmanship and the roping were doing fine. Ditto for the language. But all was not well.

Each day, visitors came to Maya's home. Conferences were held. With Jul officiating, and Maya interpreting to Odin, it became apparent to all that the Brons, at least, were at the end of their tether. Their life, their customs, their mores, their thinking: all these were a part of their man-made sun. That sun was misbehaving. Whether it was simply playing out or whether the blasts from the world above were speeding its departure, one thing was certain. Living was becoming intolerable.

Meanwhile, Jack learned, the majority of the people were going about their pleasant ways. It was a peculiar civilization, a strange mixture of Epicurean and Spartan. One man sent word that he would not be at a meeting because he had suddenly decided it would be more interesting to hunt a tiger. Noiseless machines processed most of the Brons' food. Quick-frozen, it was delivered by tube to each kitchen by merely dialing a catalogue number. Machines kept the houses and streets clean. Machines kept up the lawns, polished the marble, trimmed the trees. Yet, no person except a convalescent or a very old invalid would have been seen in one of their little powered vehicles that looked something like a boardwalk chair.

These thousands of tiny machines took their energy from the sun. Now, with the sun no longer steady, they were playing out. Jack had suggested a return to a gasoline-powered motor. They looked at him with horror. The noise and the stench, not counting the ultimate effect of vibrations on the roof above them, were abhorrent. Records showed that the little sun was 22 percent behind its energy throw-out for the past six months. Duels had increased; others crimes, mostly crimes of passion, were on the upgrade. A small group had banned themselves together, pledging mutual suicide. Another, still smaller, had taken to the temples (which were beautiful places for prayer) and had listened to a man who called himself "The Prophet Mim." At first this had been thought a good idea, until the Prophet Mim suddenly demanded a palace, a harem, and an annuity from the council. Examination revealed that Mim's interest in religion was so exaggerated that he must be pronounced insane.

The dwarfs were fatalists and refused to be annoyed by the turn of events. They were here merely because of Jul, who was an old friend of Maya's people. Jack Odin gathered that they had little love for the Brons, nor the Brons for them. They merely tolerated each other. Moreover, the Neeblings were used to annoyances. They and their flocks expected to survive somehow—in the hills, in the caves, in the sides of the cliffs. They merely shrugged at the question. They were a very old people, and they were sure that a remnant would come through. Besides, they were firm believers in the Old Norse Pantheon.

Not so with the Brons. They had known what it was to lose a home; now, faced with the same problem once more they were beginning to despair. At first, Odin had thought their tale of coming from a planet of another sun was mere moonshine. But the dwarfs had assured him that such was the case. Moreover, there were a few other facts to be considered. First, the strength of the Brons. Few of the men weighed over one-fifty, but they were fully as strong as Odin. Even Maya, slight as she was, had strength and endurance that both plagued and amazed him. Second, they had copies of ancient photographs. Maya showed him one. A purple-black square of the solar system. The sun with all its planets, and forsaken, ice-shrouded Pluto nearest to the viewer. Assuming that it was not a fake, here was unmistakable proof. It was a weird, lonely picture, with other suns blinking in the background like diamond points, and the changeless purple-black of space behind the suns and worlds like funereal velvet. Then there was another picture: the Earth, a half-globe nearly filled it, and there was the North American Continent joined to Eurasia by a vast land bridge. And out there where the curve of this world met the Pacific was the shadow of another continent. These were either forgeries or priceless, but why would anyone take such pains to fashion a fraud? Unless the Brons despised the world above so much that they had created their legends, and the proof of these legends, in order to disclaim their kin.

Perhaps Gunnar was right.

Only the Norns knew how they had woven the warp and woof of the past. Only they knew what skeins they would use for the future.

Jack Odin was still sitting there when Gunnar returned on the run. Half asleep and dreaming about a pair of golden eyes, Odin awoke to find the dwarf shaking him. He had never seen Gunnar so excited before.

"Up…up…Nors-King. The signals are flashing. The reading is higher than it has ever gone. We are in for The Long Night. Tighten your belt. Take up your sword. Oh, you fools—" These last words were addressed to the still calm sky as Gunnar shook his fist at the world above and all the races of men that cluttered it up.

Odin got to his feet, still dreaming. "Hurry, Jack," Gunnar urged. "Hurry. Wait at the gate for me. It may come any minute now."

Gunnar ran into the house, short legs flying. Odin heard him call to Jul and Maya, telling them to stay there and bar the doors. He returned on the run, carrying a blazing faggot above his head. He looked so incongruous with his ancient torch in broad daylight and his huge sword almost tripping his ankles that Odin laughed.

"Laugh at me," Gunnar yelled. "Laugh, you fool. But when the Long Night hits stay close by Gunnar. Eh, if you can fight you will get your fill. On the double now. To the shore."

Jack Odin trotted beside him and tried to apologize for his

laughter. "Listen, little giant of a man, if there is going to be fighting, why don't we stay back there and defend Maya? Are we going to fight for a shore that does not concern us?"

"Maya can fight for herself. The house is strong as a fort. But if the Long Night comes, and the gauges show that it is coming, there will be things on the beaches and things from the jungle that will frost your hair. Run, Jack Odin. Oh, those idiots up above. A man has enough to worry about in this world without drawing bad neighbors."

Soon they caught up with a little group of armed men with torches, all of them trotting excitedly toward the beaches. A siren began wailing. Beep-beep-beep—A silence and then two quick beep-beeps that nearly burst Jack's eardrums.

They came to the beach. Men were there, lighting huge bonfires. Odin stood and watched the flames as they leaped into the dark sky. For a moment his mind wandered, and as he stared into the flames he envisioned the striking figure of Maya standing there in all her beauty, staring back at him. The men were spreading the fires rapidly now. Already, they had fired the low, wooden piers.

The siren screamed again. Then, before the last "beep" was out, the sun above them went black and the siren was cut off. They were in pitch dark now, save for the bonfires and the burning piers. The blackest night that Odin could ever remember, rimmed by red flashes, with a strange, growing chill in the air that seemed to press down upon his shoulders.

"The Long Night lasted seven hours before. Stay at my side, Odin," Gunnar told him firmly. "Hell comes from the deep—"

Already, Odin was beginning to sense the fear and the cold that was about them. Opal's nights had been fixed, with a ghostly moon and a host of stars. But this was the blackness of an inner cave, the complete lack of light which one experiences in a tunnel when the power is suddenly cut off. The air was growing colder, but the chill that bit into him was more than the loss of heat. It was old, born of the first men's terror as they crept through ancient caverns while the things of the night screamed at the cave mouth.

There was now a wall of men at the beachhead. Gunnar and Odin took their places and stood side by side near the dancing shadows of a fallen but still blazing pier. "Watch. Out there." Gunnar cautioned as he pointed seaward. "Is there a wave coming in?"

Jack shielded one side of his face from the flames and strained his eyes. There was nothing to be seen but the darkness, and a thin line of flames stretching into the night from one pier which had nearly burned out.

Then he saw it. A wave—but neither of foam nor water. The things of the deep were coming to land. He saw one huge snakelike head, thrust high above the wave, its mouth opened in fear. Another, an armored thing, was striking to left and right as it cleared a path. Huge turtles, serpents, something that looked like a gator but drove forward with razor-edged flippers. Small things; wriggling things; huge, bellowing things; slashing things; striking things! They came on in one great wave of fear. The dark was filled with their sound. And the men at the beachhead braced themselves and called to each other as they waited for this hurricane of flesh and claw and fang to strike.

It struck.

After that there were hours upon hours of striking and thrusting, dodging, falling back, and rushing forward. Jack Odin's arms ached. The things of the sea came on and on. Fear-crazed, they bellowed and screamed. There was nothing to do but slash and hack at that wriggling, striking wall, while Gunnar swung his broadsword as though he was flailing his barley and kept up a weird, blood-curdling war cry. Heads were lopped off. Talons and flippers were severed. Once a huge serpent thrust its head toward them. Gunnar split its skull and the thing fell back into the water, churning it to bloody foam and taking others with it as it died. The armored things were worse. One had to thrust at their open mouths and try to keep hilt and hand away from those flashing teeth. The little things got under foot. Odin's standing-place became a pool of slime and blood and quivering flesh. Even the things that breathed water were caught in that wave of fear and came ashore to flop and die and add their stench to the night's horror.

Hour after hour the things came on. Hour after hour the men slashed and hacked. The defending wall grew thinner. Once, from the corner of his eye, Jack Odin saw a long neck flash out and a gaping mouth dodged a sword-thrust and took a warrior by the shoulder. Flesh and bone crunched as the thing tossed the man high. But Jack had little time to watch the battle. It was a matter of facing straight ahead and hacking and thrusting away. Or, occasionally, dodging to either the left or right to help Gunnar and the fighter who stood at his other side. Though in this case, it was Gunnar who came to his rescue, most of the time. The stout dwarf with the huge arms and the long sword was drenched with slime and blood. Something had raked him across his face, and a gruesome sea lizard had got its fangs deep into his thigh before they had killed it. But Gunnar was enjoying himself.

Between war cries, he gasped out his encouragement.

"There...Nors-King. Oh, that was a good thrust. Swing, man, swing. There...strike and lop. Oh, you would. Well—" This spoken, as he slashed the throat of a mailed thing that looked like nothing Odin had ever seen before. Then he would roar out his old Norse war cry and cheer them on as they faltered. "On...on. Oh, it is a good fight. Not a weakling in the line. And all of them swinging. Shoulder to shoulder. Kill and kill and kill. Oh, this is good. Like the tales of the old-ones, when gods and men stood up against the giants. Fight."

Behind them reinforcements waited and threw wood upon the fires.

The man to Odin's left was panting. "If there was only some light in the sky. Even a star—"

And Gunnar roared back. "What matters it, man? If the stars are gone we can still fight. Though the blackness take form like the dragon of darkness and coils itself about Gunnar—why, then, Gunnar will still fight." He began to chant an old song: "Oh, the ravens will feast tomorrow, and some good lads will lie dead, and there will be rejoicing and weeping, and the gods will drink deep, knowing that a man can still stand sturdy on his own two legs and fight."

"Save your breath, little man," Odin warned. "Here comes something that looks like a boxcar."

"A boxcar? Oh, I remember. Well, it does not matter." Gunnar was drunk from fighting.

At times there was a lull. As the fires behind the line leaped higher the onrushing wall of things drew back. At times the shallows were so filled with dead and dying that the frantic beasts could not come forward, but stayed yards away, bellowing, screaming, hissing, feeding.

Then a wave would clear the beach and the creatures of the deep would come on blindly.

So the fighting went. And so the Long Night passed. There was a flicker of light. Then a glow in the sky above them. And quite suddenly the sun was blazing in the loft.

The things of the deep stopped their charge. Rid of their fear-madness, they circled about and headed out to sea. Odin watched them go until they vanished, a long, shadowy wave rippling in the distance.

Then Gunnar and Odin walked away from the dead and

the stench. They fell upon the sand and lay there gasping.

Rested, Gunnar got to his feet. "Up, Jack, up. There is much to do. We must see how the others fared against the things of the jungle. Maya and Jul may need us. Oh, it was a good fight. There has been too much talk of dying. Last night Gunnar lived."

"But why did the things keep coming on?" Odin asked. "Was it the complete lack of light that maddened them?"

"I don't know. I am only a soldier and herdsman. Jul says that when the sun goes out there are disturbing rays left in the night. What does it matter? They came and we held them back. Up man, take up your sword. There may be things skulking through the streets," Gunnar said.

They went back through the town. Everywhere was wreckage. Carnage and blood. Here and there were the bodies of men, and torn carcasses of animals littered the streets. Tigers and ape-things mostly. But even tiny, furry things had gone mad during the night.

Gunnar and Odin found the body of a man sprawled over a dead tiger. Even in death he still pressed the haft of his knife against the beast's side. Crews were already busy cleaning the streets and gathering up the dead.

A woman was weeping over the torn body of a man. And as they went on, Jack Odin thought:

"Then, for all its years, this land is no better than mine. Bloodshed and tears. The fighters rejoicing over their victory, and the women weeping for their dead."

CHAPTER SIX

FOR two weeks the people of Valla—men, women and children—were at work rebuilding the damage of that long and terrible night.

The dwarfs sent help from the outlands. Sawmills and

quarries, abandoned and overgrown by vines, were reopened and for a time Valla was a place of noise and workmen. Odin fancied himself a good hand with the hammer and saw, and he worked on the piers. As for the other buildings that were damaged, they were rebuilt by artisans, with countless man-hours allotted to sculptors and artists. Shrubs and trees were planted. The trampled flowerbeds were rebuilt. Indeed, Odin learned, the landscape gardener held a high position of respect in the world of Opal.

Once he went with Maya to a funeral. It was a simple affair. As the many beautiful temples in the city proclaimed, there was only The One, and men should worship him as they pleased. There were a few words of tribute to the dead man, who had fallen during the fighting that night. Then a minute of silent prayer and the body was committed to the earth.

"For," Gunnar explained, "he now knows more about the One and the world beyond then we do. For us to say any more to the dead would be like a child trying to explain an element to a scientist."

On another afternoon, Maya took him to the Tower of the Physicians. They were mending the scars of the wounded. One man who had lost an arm was being given a new one. A child who had developed a tremor during that awful night was being cured. The repair of flesh and bone and the shaping and mending of the brain and nerves, these were the practices of the physicians of Opal. There was no sickness. An operation for a tumor or an infection was unknown. After being introduced to some of the doctors, Jack told them of his schooling and limited practice. They were amazed. One even suggested that he was joking. That the human body could be attacked and even destroyed by microbes was unbelievable. Their theory was that healthy flesh was immune to the poison of germs. There were no dentists in Opal. If a person lost a tooth from an accident, the physicians merely planted a tooth-bud in the gum by means of a delicate operation and in a short while a new tooth was growing.

Then the sound of the hammer and saw was gone. Valla looked even more beautiful than ever. The city returned to its old listless beauty.

But Jack Odin sensed that things were going on under the surface of this quiet little city. There were more groups upon the streets, talking quietly and excitedly. He knew the language well enough now. After that night's fighting, most of the people welcomed him. But a few still gave him cold glances as he passed.

At last Grim Hagen agreed to put his cold rage aside and meet with Maya and Jul. The result of their conference was a call for a gathering of all the people's representatives at the Council Tower the following day.

After Grim Hagen departed, Maya fell weakly into a chair and buried her face in her hands. "All this work and so little done. Nothing agreed upon. No plans—"

"But you and Jul have worked hard enough," Odin said, "while Grim Hagen has been sulking in his tent. I have been of no help at all. Why, I've even made things worse for you. Better take back the key you gave me, Maya."

"That too will be decided tomorrow. But they will accept you, Jack. I know they will. My people are fair. There must be some way out. Grim Hagen's idea of destruction is impossible—"

"Some day Grim Hagen's going to get it."

"Jack," she asked softly, "do you think the people up there would ever accept me? Or would I ever learn to like them? We could go back, you and I. But, no, that would be a coward's way. To leave them here—" She began to cry.

"There, now." He patted her shoulder. "I've said all along that there is no problem. You will be welcome up there. Everyone will."

"Perhaps. But we have centuries of fixed thinking behind us. There is not a person on the street who doesn't think that the world up above is an inhospitable place, filled with weaklings and idiots, dedicated to dullness and mediocrity, the nations armed to the teeth and always fighting. How could we ever overcome that—"

"You and your people are great hands at talking about individualism. I think it is a problem for each individual. Now, take you, for instance. Maya, you could go back with me. The two of us could work things out—"

She got to her feet and put her arms around his neck. Then, standing on tiptoe, she kissed him. "There!" she said, backing away, tears still shining in her eyes. "That is for saying such nice things to me, Jack Odin. But it cannot be. It would be a selfish thing for us to do. Besides, you underestimate Grim Hagen. He is a destroyer—"

But Odin stepped forward and took her in his arms and kissed her until the tears turned to laughter—and for the moment the troubles that beset the world of Opal were forgotten.

The next day he went with Maya to the Council Tower. It was one of Valla's most resplendent buildings. The massive doors to the Tower were black marble with thick panes of glass, which were so clear that one had to touch them to prove that they were there. The entire facade of the Tower consisted of twelve-foot squares of silver framed in the same black marble. Each silver square contained a bas-relief showing some chapter in the history of the Brons and Neeblings.

Entering, Odin looked up to see that there were no floors

within the Tower. High above, at least six hundred feet above, was a ceiling so cunningly contrived that one seemed to look at the sky where wisps of white clouds floated along. On the far side of the ground floor was a dais with five huge chairs sitting in a line at one side and twenty chairs ranged together on the other side. Between the entrance and the dais were row after row of chairs. The floor slanted downward so that each spectator could have a view of the dais. To right and left, a circular staircase went up the sides of the walls, and at twenty-foot intervals were balconies shaped like fluted shells. The newels to these staircases were chromium, and leaves and acorns were so cunningly carved about them that they gave the appearance of tall trees growing up to the sky.

The Tower was a masterpiece of art and architecture. Surely it would seat every adult in Valla.

Jul, Maya and Jack Odin went forward and took their places on three of the five huge chairs. Odin protesting. Soon Grim Hagen, dressed in black and scarlet, took the fourth seat and gave them a black scowl.

After he was seated, twenty old men—four of them dwarfs—filed onto the dais, bowed, and took their seats at the other side. The Tower began to fill. The chairs below them were soon taken. Twin streams began climbing the stairways and flowing out upon the balconies.

At last the doors were closed. A huge man in a tight-fitting black cloak walked out upon the dais. He placed a slug-horn to his lips and blew one blast. Then he announced that the High Council of the cities and outlands of Brons and Neeblings of the World of Opal was now in session. That the Low Council of the cities and plains had been seated. That the High Council with one member absent was ready to consider. Then he began a chant which seemed as old as time. It was filled with admonishments. And it closed with the plea that if any man, Neebling or Bron, had been imprisoned since two wanings of the sun without a hearing, now let the friends and relatives of that man step forth and be heard.

No one came forward. Indeed, the chant appeared to be a formality, born of causes won so long ago that no one paid any attention to its meaning.

"—And now, the High Council and the Low Council are here to consider the welfare of all. And may the just and the unjust attend to their decisions…"

There was a final ear-splitting blast, followed by the triumphant words: "The Councils of the Brons and Neeblings are now in session."

Odin was looking at the empty chair. "It is for the Chief Scientist," Maya whispered. "In two hundred years the Scientists have not sent a delegate."

Grim Hagen got to his feet.

He did not speak loudly, but his words were heard in the upmost balcony. "The special meeting has been called for many reasons. However, before it may continue, we must consider a new member. This man!" He pointed to Odin with a gesture that plainly showed his contempt. All the while, he was mockingly playing the part of one who sticks strictly to rules of order. "This man," he repeated, "has been seated upon instructions of Jul and Maya. Neither I nor the Scientist have voted—"

Maya rose to her feet, her golden eyes blazing, her dark curls tossing. "The Scientists have not voted for centuries," she retorted. "And you were unconscious at the time. Two votes of the only three who were available makes a majority. This man, Jack Odin, has been duly appointed."

Grim Hagen started a hot reply, but Jul interrupted. "The matter has been questioned. It has been talked abroad. Arguments are useless. We will now leave the matter to the people."

"But this man is an outlander—a creature from the upper world." Grim Hagen was sputtering.

"This man fought for us a few nights ago," Maya answered haughtily. "Jul and I have given him the key because he is from the upper world, which must soon be concerned with our worries whether we wish so or not—"

There were cries of: "Maya is right. A fighter like her father. Yes, he fought. Fought like a wildcat—"

And dissenting remarks such as: "We want no ape from the outlands on our council. Take him away. He comes after Maya, and doesn't give a bowstring for all of us—"

Jul silenced the murmuring. "We will vote now—by voice. Let each man and woman speak up. Shall the man from the world above be one of the council? Those who are for the question may speak."

They spoke. There was a roar of applause. It echoed from roof to balcony. "Yea."

The applause died. Jul spoke again. "And those who are against the question may speak."

There was a scattering of Nays, hissings, and catcalls. Quite noticeable, but nothing like the applause Odin had just received.

Jul smiled at Grim Hagen. "There, my friend, they have spoken, and Jack Odin is now one of us. Shall we continue now with the problems of the day?"

Grim Hagen bowed sardonically. "Please do, my friend." Venom dripped from the last word.

Jul ignored him. "We are in trouble—dire trouble. As you know, we sent a delegation to the world above. I myself was one of that delegation. But it was mismanaged..." He paused to bow to Grim Hagen, whose black scowl was growing blacker, "...and we accomplished little in that attempt."

"We accomplished nothing," Grim Hagen retorted.

"Now, since the Long Night of two weeks ago, it becomes vital that we decide upon some course to follow, for our affairs are going from bad to worse. First, we will speak. Then, the Lower Council will give any suggestions that it can think of. And last, let anyone in attendance speak out if he has anything worthwhile to say. But one thought. I am an old man, and my advice is for us to consider our honor. I would rather go down honorably than to live with the fires of hate and guilt consuming me until nothing but ashes is left of life. First, we will hear from Grim Hagen—"

Grim Hagen's supporters set up a burst of applause as he advanced to the center of the dais. Odin had to admit that the man had a wonderful self-assurance about him, and was a gifted public speaker.

Grim Hagen bowed. "My friends, there is but one immediate answer to our troubles. The world above is divided. It is a sickly race. And, certainly, it has caused us much grief. Their atomic tests have almost destroyed our sun. We have lived here for ages without bothering them, but now we have no choice. I say, let us gather our weapons, the old, terrible weapons—and destroy them. Living with them has become impossible. That is all."

There was another round of applause. Then a vote was taken on Grim Hagen's suggestion. It was voted down, although Odin thought uneasily that there were far too many in favor of the idea.

Jul next announced his plan. He pointed to the empty chair.

"How long has it been since a Scientist sat with us? Not in my time." He shook his head. "And yet the Scientists have one of the keys and it is they who own the Treasure House where the Old Ship is lying. We have had so little to do with the Scientists these last years that perhaps I should tell the younger ones what I know of the land of Orthe-Gard.

It is another peninsula like our own, far across the sea. Its people are Brons, but they do not think like you. They are Philosophers and Scientists. They live for thinking, and some day they hope to solve the riddle of the universe. They do not trust us, because we are fun loving, because we sometimes shed blood. And yet, they are your brothers, and they have one of the keys. And, by the old law, Orthe-Gard and the Treasure House is theirs. Now, I will tell you of the Treasure House, for I was there many times in my youth. Centuries of Brons' and Neeblings' work went into its building. It is greater than any tower we know. It has over a hundred floors, but for nearly thirty stories it is built flush against the side of the precipice—for a reason. Set within the precipice is a tunnel. There are the old treasures of the Brons and the Neeblings. And there is the Old Ship—the indestructible ship that brought your people to this planet so long ago. And there are the treasures of the sea. For this tunnel goes out onto the sea floor. It is sealed by doors as large as this tower. Our people set them there long and long ago. Now the treasure house is generally open, but the door to the tunnel is fastened by five locks. That is the reason for the five keys."

Jul paused and looked at his audience expectantly.

"I propose that we four go to Orthe-Gard and confer with the Scientists. They may know how to save our little sun. Or, failing that, we can determine if the old ship can be readied for departure. Just in case—"

The listeners began their applause before he could bow. Much to Odin's surprise, Grim Hagen rushed forward and endorsed Jul's scheme.

The Low Council too was unanimous in their endorsement. And, after anticipating hours of squabbling, Jul, Maya, and Odin found themselves on their way home within less than thirty minutes of their arrival at the Tower.

CHAPTER SEVEN

JACK ODIN and Maya were leaning upon the rail of a white ship that slid noiselessly and slowly through the low waves of a sparkling sea.

Behind them, sprawled out upon easy chairs were Jul, White Owl and Gunnar. White Owl and Jul were asleep. The little giant was looking up at the sky, lazily awaiting something to happen. Now and then he stole a look at the two at the rail and smiled.

Not far away a sea serpent, with its head and several coils of its long body thrust out of the water was pacing them. It seemed to be a peaceful creature now—far different from the things of its kind that had rushed the beaches that night. A few birds sailed overhead, their wings motionless as they glided with the barest trace of a breeze. Flying fish played in the water, and once a vast thing like a floating island raised its dripping body half out of the water and opened a tiny mouth at the end of a long neck to hiss at them. Then it sank from sight, leaving a fountain of spray to cascade after it. Jack looked down. Three of the things that he had learned to hate during the Long Night were wallowing near the ship, waiting for scraps. Gunnar called them fang-fish, though they appeared to be no more kin to a fish than a gator. Except for razor-edged flippers and a more elongated snout they did resemble a gator. When questioned about sharks, Gunnar had replied that no such critters were in the waters of Opal. If there had ever been, he judged, the fang-fish must have destroyed them long ago. They were ugly brutes, always hungry. Both scavengers and hunters, they were hated and loathed. Jack figured that they must breed like flies or they could never have survived. Hardly a day passed that the sailors did not kill at least a dozen.

With Maya leaning against him and holding his hand a dreamy wonder fell over Jack Odin as he looked down at that sluggish sea and thought of the billions of life-things that swarmed in the semi-tropical deep.

Then he remembered a Ph.D. he had known in Korea. The man had put his books aside to become a slovenly soldier—slovenly but handy with a book, a bottle, and a burp gun. The Ph.D. was dead now. Someone had clobbered him two days before the armistice. But in the retreat from the Yalu the Ph.D. had picked up a little jade carving of a dragon. It was a work of art, he had insisted. Also, it was the keystone of a book that he was going to write—a book that would astound the scientific world. It was the ex-professor's theory that the astronomical figures put upon the various geological periods was pure moonshine—that they had been shorter and often overlapped into the next age, refusing to die. For example, the dinosaurs. Surely they had lasted into the age of mankind or why would there be so many tales of dragons?

It now appeared that the Ph.D. and the book he would never write were correct. Those mountains of flesh with the small heads were certainly kin to the brontosaurs. And these fang-fish—not fish at all, but saurians lost out of time.

Odin shrugged his shoulders. Here, and with such a beautiful companion as Maya, and on this warm sea, aboard a noiseless ship that was barely moving, one could afford to be philosophical. Right or wrong, what difference did his dead friend's opinions matter now? And books that are never written always manage to be better than those that someone writes. Like the fish that gets away, or the girl that a man never got around to kissing—

Maya gave him a playful shove. "Come back from wherever you have been, Doctor Odin. We are alive here, you know, and if you flyaway to Dreamland, who will look after you?"

He laughed and put his arm around her shoulder. "Not dreaming. Remembering. And thinking—" Then, half-confiding, he added: "Those things down there are supposed to be dead ages ago. They are supposed to be extinct."

She shivered. "I wish they were. But can't we talk of more pleasant things?"

"Sure. Cabbages and kings for instance. Or queens. Now, if you could forget your real or fancied responsibilities to this world, we could go back to my home and get married. I could open up an office and trot to it every day—and woe to any patient who got sick and called me out at night. You could join the bridge club, and maybe we could make the country club. We could buy all kinds of junk, and make a down payment on practically everything. We would be quite happy and quite dull. You could sit across from me each morning at the breakfast table and pour my coffee while I read the morning paper and find out just what international dither we are going to be shook up about today."

She pouted. "I would not. You would look at me or I would never get out of bed—"

"I wouldn't tolerate a late sleeper in the house—"

"What are we talking about?" It was Gunnar. He had slipped out of his chair and was standing behind them with a gleam of merriment in his eyes.

"Eh? Oh, the international situation," Jack hastened to assure him.

Gunnar laughed. "Then the international situation hasn't changed much since I was a young soldier and was courting Freida."

He laughed and winked and gave Odin a playful dig in the ribs. "And how do you like our ship?" he asked.

"We have faster and noisier ones."

"More speed. More noise. You go places faster so you can return faster. You go so fast and hurry so much that you are like the boy who got the tiger by the tail. They were running in a circle and going so fast that the boy wasn't sure whether he was chasing the tiger or the tiger him. But he hoped that someone would come along before the race was over."

It was a peculiar ship. Sparkling white, with neither sail nor smoke. Jack understood that it was powered by huge batteries that were daily charged by the sun. There was hardly a sound from it. No vibration at his feet. They sailed dreamily along at a pace of five miles per hour. No more. No less. Always, the five miles. The sea was so calm that there was no lurching. Odin had never been a good sailor, but he had seen lakes back home with higher waves than these.

They had been voyaging for three days now. Two more and they would dock at the home of the Scientists. Jul had assured him that he was in for one of the Marvels of the World. The Treasure House. It had taken centuries of Brons and Neeblings to build it. Higher than the Empire State Building, it was one elaborately carved cube, set against the precipice wall for thirty floors. After that, it became a faery cathedral going up and up, always growing smaller, until at last one golden spire with its lesser spires below it, reached up into the sky like a prayer and caught at the trailing clouds.

"Carvings. Jewels. Gold. Silver. Ah, lad," Jul had grown reminiscent. "What would I give to be young again and to see the Treasure House for the first time!"

During the long days, Maya and Jul had taken turns with the books, teaching Odin more and more about Opal. Gunnar had set aside three hours per day for the sword and the thon. That had still left a great many hours, though not near enough, to be alone with Maya.

Grim Hagen and one of his lieutenants were on board but they stayed in their cabins. Once a day they came upon the deck for a bit of swordplay. Grim Hagen was good, Odin admitted. Plenty good.

Grim Hagen spoke curtly to Maya and the dwarfs. He looked through Odin when he came topside. Odin had gritted his teeth. Some day—some day soon—he would get his hands on that arrogant fool, and all the Physicians wouldn't be able to put him together again.

So the hours passed. Quietly. Calmly. It was like a dream come to life, or the remembrance of past things. An unhurried quiet. A faery ship on a faery sea with a faery sky above them. Troubles and panic might have lain all around them, but these were ignored. When they reached the land of the Scientists there would be time enough to talk over their troubles. Meanwhile, life was good. They became like the birds who perched on deck for a short spell. There were weary hours of flight behind them and they did not know what lay ahead. But here was rest and quiet. There was nothing to do but look at the world around them. And the world was good—

It was but a few moments before the waning of the sun. Odin and Maya, after pages of lessons, had returned to the rail. Gunnar and White Owl were fencing upon the deck— White Owl silent and nimble, Gunnar strong and loud.

"It has been a good day," Maya was saying as she leaned her cheek against Odin's shoulder. Such a beautiful day. If God should give this as the last day to the world, then no one should complain."

Odin had been looking far off toward the west. A bank of clouds had settled down upon the sea and little flashes of heat lightning were twinkling across them.

"Maya," he cried. "See there." He pointed toward the

cloudbank.

"What, dearest. I don't see anything."

And then the little sun gave its warning flicker and dwined to the ghost of a moon, which was already writing its old runes of silver upon the sea.

Maya shivered, and clung to him. "What was it, Jack—"

He rubbed his eyes. "I couldn't tell. I can't be sure. Just before that cloudbank settled down I thought I saw a ship over there. Then other ships. All close together. Many ships—"

She laughed. "It was only a cloudbank. See, there are no lights over there. And with the going of the sun our ship is alive with lights. It is the law—"

Then she kissed him. It was such a long kiss that he forgot about ships and cloudbanks—

CHAPTER EIGHT

THE next two days were uneventful. Odin and Gunnar watched for ships but none were seen. On the fifth day there were more birds about them, and they passed several beautiful little Islands.

Then "Orthe-Gard Ho!" came a cry from the lookout. They rushed to the forward rail, old Jul standing proudly by Odin to watch his face at the first sight of the Treasure House.

Before them with a rising mist above its housetops was Orthe-Gard. It was a fine city, Jack thought, but no better than Valla. Standing apart from him and his group were Grim Hagen and Hagen's lieutenant. Odin watched the man for a second. As they neared Orthe-Gard, Grim Hagen's face became a set sardonic mask, and his black eyes blazed as though at long last he had found a treasure and was reaching forth to take it.

Then the mist began to rise, and back of the city of Orthe-Gard, over against the cliff-wall was the Treasure House. At first Jack could see only the lower part of it. An immense cube, even as Jul had told him, with carved windows and balconies high up—and the entire front covered with inlay of gold and silver and marble. The mist rose higher and Jack gasped for breath. Up and up it went, always tapering. Spire after spire flashed in the sun as the mist withdrew. It was all gold and rosy marble at the midway point. And as the mist lifted he saw that the marble predominated, deepening in color, until the very top of the tower was like a sunset—with one needle of gold still reaching upward toward the sky.

Maya thrust a pair of field glasses into his hand. They brought the tower into easy view, and Jack marveled at the carvings and inlay. There was not a square foot of space that had not been worked by a master hand—no, millions of master hands! Stones of all colors flashed, blazed and smoldered there. Some of the gold and silver carvings must have weighed tons. Jul had prepared him for the sight, in a way, but this was far beyond Jul's description. More massive at the base than any building he had ever seen, taller than any on Earth, it was an architecture where strength and beauty were so skillfully woven together that not a line was lost. Tower after tower, soaring upward, with each one adding a note to the symphony of color. Even the gold filigree work on the outside balconies, which at this distance looked like fine lace, appeared to blend into the whole of that cathedral of stone and gems and precious metals.

Jack Odin shook his head in wonder. It defied the imagination. Not even the exaggerated tales of Ormuz or the fancied city of Cibola, which had been a lonely dream in men's hearts, could equal the strength and beauty of this tower.

He watched it, awe-struck, until they docked. A

bespectacled man in a pale-green robe was the leader of the small group that came to meet them. He was a trifle stooped and his hair was iron gray—but his face had a youngish look.

"Welcome," he said, smiling quietly. "I am Wolden—the one you call the Chief of the Scientists and Philosophers. We do not use the term here. Here, I am merely Wolden. No one is chief—"

They acknowledged his greeting. He remembered Jul, and the two exchanged a few words about their families. Then he introduced the rest of the party.

"My son, Ato." A tall, young man with a short sword at his side stepped forward. He looked more like the young men of Valla than the men of Orthe-Gard. The rest of the party consisted of scientists and thinkers whose work had won them a place in the councils of Orthe-Gard. Several wore glasses. Odin had not seen a pair in Valla—not even Jul had needed them.

As they went through the clean streets, Jack noted that there were fewer pretentious buildings. Here were more shops and meeting places. They passed several bookstalls. These were as new to Odin as the spectacles. In Valla the books were hand-me-downs. There were no libraries, and though many of the editions he had seen were works of art few had been read of late.

Wolden kept up a flow of talk, as pleasant and unimportant as that of any experienced diplomat. "After you have refreshed yourselves we have planned a dinner. I am sure you will enjoy it. We have developed some fruits here far different from the parent stock. And after that, as custom decrees, we must try the locks of the Tower." He laughed and spoke aside to Odin, "It is an ancient custom. An atom blast could not wreck the door—"

"It is more than a custom," Grim Hagen announced sharply. "There has been no inspection in years. How do we know that the old treasures are there?"

His rude comment threw a cloud over the party. Ato looked at Grim Hagen, frowned, and his right hand fell lightly to the handle of his sword.

But Wolden laughed. "The people of Orthe-Gard have kept the treasures for nearly twenty-five thousand years, Grim Hagen, I am sure that in the last ticking of time there has been no pilfering—"

Grim Hagen remained stiff-necked. "Time is ticking out," he retorted sullenly. "And time has changed—"

Wolden smiled sadly. "Yes, changes come and go. But if we had two more centuries, free and unbothered, we could prove to you that time does not exist."

He sighed and tried a half-cheerful smile. "That word *if.* It streams through the universe like a flash of light. And it leaves the stardrifts behind it. It closes its books on bugs and men and suns like an old accountant. But, once mastered—" He sighed again. "Well, never mind. We of Orthe-Gard welcome you, and as our friend says: "Time is ticking out.""

The little party from Valla had docked at Orthe-Gard near the tenth hour. Wolden gave them rooms in his home. Later, they had been given a quick tour of the city—in little powered cars, for the people of Orthe-Gard did not share Valla's contempt for vehicles. At one o'clock they had banqueted and had met more of the city's dignitaries. There had even been a few speeches. All as dull as the ones that had bored Odin to distraction in the world above.

Now, at three, they stood in front of the door of the Treasure House. Craning their necks they looked up and up at that wealth of carvings and metalwork—until they grew dizzy and looked back at the door in continued awe.

Wolden and Ato led them into the tower. Here, the scientists and philosophers had gathered the wealth of Opal.

Paintings, sculptures, designs, room after room, corridor after corridor. They saw several reading rooms as large as most libraries. Students and teachers wandered through the halls, talking low to one another. There were fossils and pictures taken from Jack's world. There were displays of ancient machines and tools.

Once, Grim Hagen paused before a small helicopter. "Has the motor been removed from this?" he asked. His contempt for these devices was plain enough.

"Yes," Wolden sighed. "In accordance with an old agreement. An agreement that was a mistake, I fear—"

"It was no mistake," Grim Hagen scowled. "These would have softened the race—"

"Perhaps. Let the race have thews of steel and die here," was Wolden's soft-spoken reply.

Ato tried to change the subject. "There are thousands of rooms here. Perhaps you will have time to see them all. Right now, we are taking the most direct route to the door."

"It's like some old university and the Smithsonian combined," Odin said admiringly.

"I have heard of the Smithsonian," Ato answered. "Some day, I would like to see it."

"And you shall, my friend," Odin assured him. "All this talk of death and not daring to associate with the world above is nothing but graveyard music. All of you have got spooky down here. What you need is more air and a real sun above you—"

Grim Hagen sneered once more. "You have seen only a few of our treasures. Imagine what that pack of rats up there would do with them. The blood they would shed— Within a week the world above would turn this into a shambles."

Odin could feel the blood surging to his face. "Grim Hagen," he told the dark man savagely, "some day I am going to kill you. I have had enough of your insults, but this is no time to fight. Don't push me—"

Grim Hagen bowed. "Any time, Odin. Any time—"

"Boys. Boys!" Jul shook his head—

In an embarrassed and infuriated silence they came to the door that led out into the tunnel.

Here were the five locks that Odin had heard so much about. The door was massive enough, as large as the door to a good-sized hangar.

Five keys were ceremoniously produced. The doors swung open. Maya clung to Odin as they looked forward into a gulf of shimmering light.

Here was the tunnel, growing larger as it receded from them. Set into the rock walls was something more than phosphorous. It glimmered and glittered. Sparks flashed from it into the timeworn air. And Odin found himself thinking: This was the way it was in the beginning, with light forming itself from darkness, and the atoms flashing from nothingness, to press together for a million years until their weight exploded into suns and worlds, and God looked upon them and found them good.

Before them was a little truck without a top—larger, but somewhat resembling a pickup of the world above. Its wheels were set upon a track.

They took their seats and Ato pressed a button that started the truck moving upon its rails. As they moved forward the light increased. It was like moving through a panorama of the ages. To right and left were the heaped up treasures of the centuries—unclassified and jumbled together like the collection of an old antiquarian. Weapons, heaps of jewels, strange machines, statuaries, paintings, heaps and heaps of leather-bound books, gold, silver, platinum. Here was a 1918 Ford—and there was a skeleton of a tyrannosaur. Resting upon a golden dais was the Laocoon, its marble as bright as though it had been fashioned yesterday. Here an Indian blanket of hummingbird feathers that a score of Indian maids must have worked on for a decade.

Here was an exotic teocalli that must have run with blood during the reign of the Aztecs. There was a Cross set with so many gems that it was a blaze of light. An ancient Oldsmobile was resting beside a Peacock Throne that some Persian king had loved. A doctor's saddlebags leaning against a portable cobalt X-ray.

A Rembrandt which would have covered a wall and a tiny Venus by Botticelli. Guns. The guns that Jesse James might have used, and the cannon from Gettysburg. And beside them a needle-nosed thing that looked so much like death that it must have been born upon another planet.

The car moved forward slowly. The loft above them drew away. The walls receded. But always there was that spark-filled space which made all things clearly visible but cast no shadow.

On and on. And as the tunnel grew larger they seemed to plunge along a star-swept Milky Way where life and time and light had been frozen into one.

On and on. And now the roof above them was only a shimmering aurora that dripped rose and purple curtains of flame. And the sides of the tunnel were so far away that they gleamed with a misty, golden light. On and on the truck moved while the ceiling and the sides of the tunnel fled away from them.

Until at last they came to a spot where the spaceship was resting.

Odin had grown so accustomed to pictures of spaceships these last years that he had been expecting to see a huge metal cigar. But this was beyond him.

Standing at least three thousand feet into the air, it was more like a gigantic hourglass. In the center of the glass was one great bulb of gleaming-white metal. Coiled about it, up and down, around and around, were tubes of that same metal. And at random intervals these tubes passed through lesser globes of black and white. The globe in the center of the hourglass was at least a thousand feet across almost the same width as the top and base of the hourglass.

The spaceship was resting upon huge dollies which in turn had wheels set into chromium tracks—dozens of tracks that went forward into that void of shimmering light.

They went on.

Now the treasures to left and right were alien to Odin. Paintings, sculptures, weapons, they had been born upon another world under another sun. A bronze-skinned man stood with nothing but a spear against an onrushing thing which was mostly teeth and claws and thorny hide.

A nude bronze-skinned girl reclined in a garden where butterflies encircled her until she became the center of a vast flower of whirling color. A bronze Macbeth, knife in hand, walked through a corridor below his castle while the witch-woman hung to the air beside him and urged him on to his doom.

The machines and weapons scattered about had no comparison with the things of Earth. Cylinders, globes, burred ovals, things with barrels, things with needles, things with claws. An aura of the death they could deal hung over them.

Until at last they came to the end of the tunnel and there was the greatest thing that Jack Odin had seen in the world of Opal. It was a massive double-door that resembled cedar, but upon touching it Odin found it to be cold and slightly electrifying metal. They went high up, these doors, over three thousand feet. Here were five locks, as before, and the hinges upon these doors were of shining brass, and each hinge was larger than the outer gate. Mentally, Odin took off his hat to the men who had built these doors. From behind them came a murmuring as of the sea—and he thought: "To build these was a job for the gods, but to hold the sea back as they built—that would be more than the mind of man can fathom."

There was a steady murmuring, and Jul clutched at Odin's elbow and pointed off to one side. Over there was a smaller door for sending exploring parties in to the deep.

He heard Wolden say: "And now, Grim Hagen, we have kept the pledge. Here are the rails and there is the door. We still have our old escape route. We have guarded it—like men who guard a long-dead altar. For the escape route is nothing. It is merely a pathway to the old error. Had you not been so busy with your tiger hunting, we could have shown you that time and times are done. We have no patience with these things any more. That is why we have not sent a delegate to the Council. These things are dead and done with. Life and time are merely the splashing of silver drops into the pool below the fountain. The fountain itself is the pulse and the flame—changeless and beyond the ticking of time."

Grim Hagen laughed. "I prefer the tiger. Your philosophy is nothing but moonshine—"

"Not moonshine. Flames. We shall become Ideas casting our thoughts into the gulf. And the thoughts shall be like flame-winged butterflies. And there shall be no death, because there shall be no error. And eternity shall wheel about us in one vast ring of light. Today, tomorrow, and yesterday shall be like a trip to the corner store. And we shall be as gods—"

And, suddenly, Jack Odin found himself remembering an old Sunday school lesson:

"And they said, 'Go to, let us build us a city and a tower whose top may reach unto heaven.'"

And another: "—now, lest he put forth his hand, and take also of the tree of life, and eat, and live forever."

Grim Hagen laughed again.

"Now, that sounds fine indeed. But the misery of Earth is something that confounds all philosophers. And if I were a philosopher, which I am not, I would prepare for the worst. Then, if it should come, I would face it with a strong back and a good sword. Troubles beset us by the moment— happiness is a vagrant who pays us an occasional visit. I would be strong enough to turn aside any trouble caused by another man—and I would add that man's ears to the balance. You can preach about flame-winged butterflies all you wish, Wolden, but give me a stout arm and a good sword—"

For the first time, Jack Odin found himself sympathizing with Grim Hagen. And then he remembered a third Sunday school lesson: "They who live by the sword shall die by the sword."

As though sensing his thoughts Grim Hagen drew his blade and held it up toward the light-flecked ceiling. "There. The enemy of tyrants. The steel that holds the usurer away— the bar against the invader of fields. If a man cannot save himself, then the night birds sing his eulogy. If a man's wealth be maidens or gold, respect or home, this is all that keeps out the rapacious world. And it is enough."

Gunnar pointed out his error. "Grim Hagen, I could kill you in a wink and I want nothing that you have."

"Then you would be a fool," Grim Hagen snorted. "For to the victor belongs the spoils—"

"Nonsense," Maya said, stamping her foot. "You are offending our hosts."

Grim Hagen bowed. "Forgive me, my princess. I meant no offense. But the affairs of the world go ill—and I, for one, would prepare myself for the worst—"

The air near the towering gates was damp. And a dampness had fallen over the little party at the clashing of ideas.

"All the treasures are here, Grim Hagen," Wolden said stiffly. "Do you wish to take inventory?"

Grim Hagen sneered. "With so much, a guard could pilfer a thousand treasures and never be caught—"

Ato clutched at his sword. "The man from the upper world may be wrong. I may have to kill you myself, Grim Hagen."

Grim Hagen laughed. "Already, three have promised to kill me. Am I that valuable? Never mind, I am satisfied that the Scientists and Philosophers have kept the pledge. They have been too busy chasing moonbeams to take anything. Let us get out of here, for the air is damp."

And so they returned to Orthe-Gard, and found the little sun still shining in the roof above them. But for the rest of the day Gunnar was sharpening a pair of swords—one for Jack Odin, and the long broadsword for himself.

"I am not a philosopher," he said. "But the time comes when swinging steel must clash into the scales. There, my lovely," he said and held his broadsword straight out before him. "The song of the flame was frozen into your sharp steel. And only blood can release the song. For time runs out and the singer sings no more. Oh, Jack Odin, if Gunnar should go out into the dark night, think well of him, as one who loved you for the short time he knew you. And remember Gunnar, who backed down to no man."

Later, White Owl joined them. The little man was glum, "I had a dream," he told them. "The strangest dream. There was death all about me and I too was dead. And the valkyries were choosing us. The most beautiful one took White Owl. Oh, Gunnar, the threads are torn from the skein. And time has run out for us. If you live, remember the little man who stood beside you in the fighting. For my people are all dead. And I am like a wheel whose felloes are broken. The nave with its shattered spokes has rolled aside. Remember me, Gunnar, and you too, Jack Odin, for I leave no kith or kin behind me. And I dreamed that there was fighting such as we had never seen—"

"You have been drinking, little man," Gunnar assured him.

But White Owl was moody. "The wine of violence is in the air. And the honey-mead of an ancient hate and hunger still makes a man yearn to stand shoulder to shoulder with the gods. These have been my drink this day, Gunnar. The skivers of the gods are growing thin, Gunnar. They may shape a lovely gem, but White Owl will be lost among the shavings."

CHAPTER NINE

THAT night the High Council of the world of Opal met for the last time. Guards, soldiers, and advisers were all about. But, strictly speaking, the five holders of the ivory and ruby keys were there to decide.

Jack Odin had to admit that Grim Hagen dominated the meeting. Whether anyone liked the man or not, he was a forceful speaker. His hate and his distrust for the world above had grown into a passion. He had become a zealot of destruction—and zealots, right or wrong, are always hard to shout down in the councils of the world. They see no middle ground. To them, there are no shadings to any idea. They are simply one hundred percent right; those who oppose them are one hundred percent wrong. The Council was meeting in one of the lesser halls of the Treasure House. It could easily have held a thousand, but not over two hundred spectators had arrived. Many of these were already applauding Grim Hagen.

Odin wondered about that. Had the man a following in Orthe-Gard? Were these some of his own men that he had sent on ahead? Or was Orthe-Gard so lost with its scientific and metaphysical problems that it could not see the danger that threatened them?

Grim Hagen was concluding his speech: "—and are we to take our tributes of bread and salt to a world we never made? It is they who are destroying us. We have done them no harm, other than to take and preserve a few priceless treasures that were being thrown upon their junk-piles. They are many, but they are weak and divided. Within a month we could destroy their armies and fleets. Within two months we could enslave them, and put them to useful chores which they have shirked these many years."

There was scattered applause, but Jul rose swiftly to his feet in protest. "There has not been any slavery here. It was forbidden in the beginning."

Grim Hagen answered soothingly. "It would not be slavery as they have known it. Their slavery was brutal and destructive. This would be the discipline of the schoolyard. They must learn the lessons they have refused to study. They will never learn, unless they are forced to do so. Unless they have what they call a Big Brother to keep them at their studies! Under such conditions the Scientists and Philosophers could perfect their theories and inventions. I am impressed with Wolden's work upon the Time-Scheme. The suns are far away. Unless time can be folded up like a fan, these worlds will remain a life span away. Meanwhile, with men cured of their idiocies and their limitations, their fighting and their absolute refusal to think, we could have the planets colonized within a score of years. Look! There is a rock upon the dead moon that can give forth water and oxygen in abundance. Jupiter has a moon not greatly different from this world. Warmth can be given that moon. Why our ancestors chose to hide down here in a dangerous cellar, I do not know."

Maya arose now, her eyes flashing. "And who are you to criticize what they did? You—you little man who puts himself higher than the thought-out decisions of the past—? Let Jul speak."

But Jul answered: "On that matter I do not care to speak—not yet."

Grim Hagen's smile was a jeer. "He cannot speak. He knows I am right. We have lived here too long. The walls of this inner world press in upon us. The people of the upper world annoy us daily with their atom blasts. One short war and they will have set off enough of those blasts to finish the destruction of our sun. Then you will grope around here for a few days. You will become pallid, creeping things. And you will die with your useless treasures and all your learning about you. I ask you, is that a pleasant future for a race whose ancestors dared the gulf between the suns? Or is it good for the Neeblings whose fathers dared the deep caves and the things of the caves to find this world?"

"Do not worry about us Neeblings," Jul answered. "We dared the caves and the labyrinths before. We can do so again."

"I move that we vote." Grim Hagen screamed his rage and frustration. "Destruction for the upper world."

There was scattered applause. Far too much applause from such a small crowd, Odin thought.

But Wolden silenced the spectators with a wave of his hand as he got to his feet. "This plan is criminal and it is insane. It is not practical, for there would always be some remnant of men who would hide out and get you, one by one. There is something in the hearts of men that revolts against slavery—even a genteel, well-ordered slavery such as Grim Hagen proposes. You have underestimated those men up there. I can think of nothing that would unite a disordered world better than our attack. No, it is foolish. I will admit that you led a party up there, Grim Hagen, but you skulked about like a lost dog in the moonlight—"

"We did not skulk." Grim Hagen screamed.

"You were skulking when I first saw you," Jack Odin retorted.

Grim Hagen, sword in hand, was halfway around the council table when Ato and two other soldiers stepped between him and Odin.

"There will be no fighting here, Grim Hagen," Wolden warned. "Sit down—" Grim Hagen sheathed his sword, bowed politely, and obeyed.

"Now," Wolden continued. "I have a plan. The people up there are adherents to formalities. I suppose all the races of men are, lest they go back to the jungle. Some of their formalities appear foolish, but let us humor them. We have our receivers which daily pick up their messages. If the Council authorizes, we can build a good transmitter in less than twenty-four hours. Then we can talk with them and arrange for a meeting. Our delegates would go forth in their best trappings, honoring all the formalities and fol-de-rol of statecraft as those up there know it. There are reasonable men in that world, just as there are reasonable men here. And neither group has a monopoly upon fools."

"No—" Grim Hagen protested.

"I move that we vote upon the two proposals," Jul thundered.

"Good. Those in favor of Grim Hagen's proposal—"

"Aye," cried Grim Hagen, and scores in the audience shouted their approval.

"One vote." Wolden announced. "Those who are in

favor of my proposal—"

He added his own "aye" to the other three votes.

"Then it is decreed," Wolden announced solemnly. "Now, I move that we adjourn, for there is much work to do—"

But Grim Hagen was on his feet for his final speech. "This was no vote. You four had decided such before you came here. Well, it is not enough. I will take my fight to the lesser councils and to the clans and the people. This is an outrage thrown upon all the outrages of the past. They are heaped about you like scrap piles. Those ash heaps of honor and dust-bins of timidity will put forth such clumps of nettles that they will choke you and the world. Time is a tired old man, and he has grown weary of you. Grim Hagen's day dawns, and tonight you have pulled your grave-cloths about you. Oh," he sputtered in wrath. "When I am done, you will remember Grim Hagen. The Old Worm gnaws at the bases of your towers, and the pinnacles topple and fall. There comes a new day to be baptized in blood, and that day is Grim Hagen's."

Without another word he stormed out of the meeting place. His lieutenant and a few others followed.

CHAPTER TEN

JACK ODIN awoke with the distant blare of loudspeakers troubling his ears. There was a hurried knock at his door and Gunnar came in, buckling on his harness and his long sword as he came.

"Hear that," Gunnar exclaimed. Going to the window he flung it open: "There. Listen."

At first, Odin thought he was re-living the last minutes of that tempestuous scene with Grim Hagen of the night before. Grim Hagen's voice was everywhere. During the night, hundreds of loudspeakers had been installed throughout Orthe-Gard. The voice of Grim Hagen screamed and threatened:

"Surrender now, all of you. My ships are landing. Maya and the Chief Scientist are my prisoners. My men have taken the Treasure House. Surrender. All of you. There is no other chance. Surrender now, or face death from me or the world above. Grim Hagen is that which stands between you and death. Surrender now, accept me as ruler of Opal, and we will plan our attack upon the outer world. I tell you, it can be ours. And if you do not accept me, we will take you as our prisoners and leave in the spaceship. We will depart, flooding Opal when we go. You have no other choice. This message is addressed to the Brons. As for the dwarfs, they must be destroyed—regardless. Our ancestors made a terrible mistake. No two races can live together. We have harbored these snakes long enough. Kill the dwarfs and bring me the bread and salt of surrender. You have no other choice!"

Ato and White Owl came rushing into the room. "Your princess and my father are gone." Ato was breathless. "Father was right. We should have had nothing to do with the other cities. Trouble is all they have brought us. Oh, why didn't I kill that Grim Hagen? I wanted to—but I held back— And now my father is gone. Maya is gone and the keys are gone—"

"The key!" Odin, despite Gunnar's many warnings, had put his cumbersome key on a little dressing table the night before. It was gone.

"Where is Jul?" he asked—fear and rage beating at his throat.

"Not to be found," Ato answered. "There is a trace of a hypnotic gas in the house. Someone must have pumped it into the air conditioners. Why they didn't kill all of us, I do not know—unless they were hurried for time—or the warriors lost their nerve."

A quick search of the house of Wolden gave no trace of Jul, the Ancient of the Neeblings. But in the back yard, within a clump of torn and trampled hydrangeas they found his body. He had fallen over a slain Bron, and his knife was still biting into the dead man's ribs. As old as he was, Jul had accounted for himself well. It may have been that his attack upon Grim Hagen's soldiers—for they found many other tracks in the yard—had saved the lives of the few who remained in the house.

"It is the end of my dream," said White Owl. "Now, let us go forth and kill, and kill, and kill."

But Ato motioned him to silence as he turned a dial beneath a dark picture frame upon the wall. The picture came on, and they could see the docks with dozens of Grim Hagen's ships moored there, and others still arriving pouring their troops and weapons of war upon the city.

Odin was remembering: "That fleet. I did see it out there in the low cloudbanks that evening. Well, we must fight now.

White Owl, you and Gunnar stay here, while Ato and I go out—"

"What?" Gunnar asked, horrified.

"Those loudspeakers are dripping with hatred for the Neeblings. I have known such tactics before. Within a few hours, many will be convinced that the Neeblings are the cause of all their troubles."

Gunnar tightened his wide belt another notch. "Then we will go out there and see what we can do to end that trouble. Jul is dead and Maya is gone. Grim Hagen will swilk in Bron's blood before Gunnar is done."

"I saw this in my dream," White Owl was saying, looking intently at the wall as though still half-asleep. "I saw in my dream that the valkyries were coming for White Owl, but they would not want him if he did not have his dead around him. Well, it has been a good life, and I am well content. In time, I have had many jobs to do. But now there is only one task left before me…to kill. That makes things much easier. For White Owl is a simple man, wearied of too many ideas. The one remaining thought appeals to me. Gunnar, let us go, for Jack Odin and Ato here still have many thoughts—while I have but one remaining."

"No," said Ato, "we go together…we four. My father is out there somewhere. I am younger than the rest of you, but I too can kill."

"And Maya is out there too," Jack Odin replied. "What Grim Hagen has brought to the forge I will beat out, and the sparks of death will fly. I have tried to be a peaceful man, but neither world would let me. Now, if it is death they want, that is what I will give them."

So, leaving the house and the grounds empty behind them, they went out into Grim Hagen's day of blood.

The sound of the loudspeakers grew louder. And over that insane bragging—over, and over, and over, as though Grim Hagen had made a recording—was the sound of fighting.

They had not gone ten blocks before a dozen men rushed at them. They had been looting, for gold chains and jeweled charms were about their necks and arms.

At sight of the dwarfs they rushed forward. But four withdrew sheepishly when they saw Ato. The other eight came on, and Gunnar met the foremost with a sweeping blow that nearly decapitated him. The man fell, spouting blood. The remaining seven turned to flee. But White Owl cast his leather lariat and drew one back. Before the man could get his balance White Owl had cut his throat.

"The first for the Sky-Maidens," he whooped. "Gunnar, stand beside me and we will take this city for our own."

"If there is but one dry stone left, I will stand beside you, little man," Gunnar encouraged. "On...and on. Ah, this blade is thirsty, and I have been too patient. The old wrongs are no longer sleeping. My blood is boiling. Come, Ato and Odin, let us turn these streets into a shambles."

They went on, killing as they went. But, upon seeing Ato, many of the men of Orthe-Gard joined him. Within an hour they had a following of several hundred men behind them. The Neeblings were jubilant now, eager to kill any they met—and even a bit disappointed when some joined them.

The party neared the docks, and there they found that Orthe-Gard still possessed an army. There was heavy fighting going on, but the soldiers were pressing the invaders back to the sea walls.

Seeing that they were not needed, Ato veered them aside and they went back through the bloody streets toward the Treasure House. The loudspeakers were still blaring, though they destroyed a few as they went along.

By four o'clock, with at least five hundred men behind them, they neared the front of that massive building. The doors were closed. The windows were barricaded. An ominous quiet hung over it, whereas before there had been a hum of peaceful activity about this pile of silver and gold and marble. Odin remembered the students and scientists coming and going, discussing the books and the thoughts that were housed there.

"I have always been taught that it was impregnable," Ato told Odin and Gunnar as they watched from a distance. "But my father and your princess are there. Also, this Grim Hagen, the cause of all our troubles. I see nothing left except to make a direct assault."

They discussed their chances for a few minutes. But since no other choice remained, they improvised huge battering rams and the five hundred charged for the doors.

Those doors opened. The barricades behind the windows

were drawn clear.

Within five minutes time a fiery hell of destruction fell upon the attackers. A needle-nosed machine behind the doors lanced long flames at them. Something sputtered at a window and spat forth blobs of acid that melted flesh and bone. Incendiaries, bombs, machine-guns, cannons poured death upon the troops. A score of crab-like metal machines dashed out of the Treasure House and whacked and snipped until countless sword-strikes broke or overturned them.

Five minutes was all it lasted. No charge could have withstood that defense. They fell back with half their number gone and of that number many were so maimed and wounded that not one out of ten could ever fight again.

A pocket radio told Ato that the troops at the docks were holding their own. And with that news—the only encouraging news of the day—they crouched within some shattered buildings near the Treasure House and waited until night fell and a ghostly man-made moon was riding in the sky.

CHAPTER ELEVEN

ATO had done all he could. "Like children attacking a hornet's nest." He shook his head wearily. "We underestimated this Grim Hagen. Those machines were not ready for battle. He must have planned this affair for months."

"Never mind," Jack Odin assured him. "In time, I will get Grim Hagen. Even if he wins this whole world I'll get him."

Off to one side, Gunnar and White Owl had been carrying on a low conversation.

Now Gunnar came forward with a proposal.

"In the old days," he told them, "my people could enter that tower as they pleased. The upper levels were theirs. Up there are many entrances. The balconies—"

"It is over five hundred feet before there is a ledge," Ato objected. "I know how you feel, friend Gunnar. I have never liked the idea. I like it less now. The helicopters belonged to the Neeblings. It is a shame that they were taken away from you—"

Even with despair and worry gnawing at his shoulders, Jack Odin found himself thinking: "So their tales of equality and living peacefully together were all lies. Something was wrong; I knew it from the start. They were equal as long as the Neeblings knuckled down to them."

As though sensing his thoughts, White Owl broke in: "Well, the helicopters are not here. But we have the thons and we can make grappling hooks. That wall is not altogether smooth. Helping each other along, twelve stout men could climb it." He looked at Odin thoughtfully. "You are strong enough, but you are heavier than the rest. I don't know—"

Odin's eyes blazed his answer. "If that wall can be climbed, I can climb it. I would hang up there by my eyelashes for a chance at Grim Hagen—"

Ato had lost his weariness. "White Owl, Gunnar, you may be right. By the One and Only, I'll chance it. Wait, I can even add to our chances. Why hadn't I thought of it before? I must hurry back to my father's house."

White Owl went with Ato, and in less than an hour they were back with new-forged grappling hooks. Ato also brought a wide belt with him—a belt with huge black studs.

"These have hardly been tried. But I used this once when I ventured far up the cliff wall. Here," he buckled it about Odin's waist. "It is a part of my father's work on the time scheme. A by-product, you might say. But it is good for only a second. It takes a huge surge of power. And it has not been perfected. But for a second—when this stud is pressed-—he wearer is weightless. Time stops for him, and of course gravitation stops."

Gunnar was in a hurry to get started. "This is no time for discussions," he growled. "If it will work, that is the thing. We Neeblings do not need such an invention. I suggest that sixteen of the best of us try the wall. That is all the grappling hooks you beat out, little man,"—this was said to White Owl—"Did you like the number? Or did you get tired?"

"I do not get tired." White Owl shook his fist under Gunnar's nose. "Time was running out—"

There was some talk of scaling the cliff behind the Tower, but that had been smoothed and covered with glassite centuries before. So, after a few last minute instructions from Gunnar, the party crawled through the shadows to the front of the Treasure House. Sixteen of them—five dwarfs, ten Brons, and Odin—all of them carried lariats.

Half an hour later, the men were clinging to the walls like flies. Below them, a hundred feet down and shining with a ghostly light, were the sidewalks of the Tower. Odin gritted his teeth. His arms and shoulders ached. His fingers were torn. If it had not been for Gunnar they would never have got ten feet off the ground. He had gone up first, hanging on to the gold and silver work. He had gouged out places for a foothold. Searched for knobs and angles of metal work to serve as anchors for the thons. In one respect, Odin thought, they were lucky that the carvings and bas-reliefs were of gold and silver. But these metals were too soft for safety, and he would have preferred granite or steel.

But they went up. How, Jack never knew. Gunnar and White Owl practically lifted themselves by the seats of their britches. Once he heard a sharp gasp from up above. A whisper of warning, and one of Ato's men hurtled downward. Odin gritted his teeth when he heard the man hit the walk below. The Bron had not cried out. They waited to see if any of Grim Hagen's men had heard. Then, once more, they began inching upward.

At last they halted over five hundred feet above the walks. Below them, the broken bodies of four Brons were sprawled out upon those walks. Twisted shadows, with bloodstains creeping away from them. Not one had cried out. This night, Odin's patience with the Brons had worn thin, but Lord, they had courage. Too much pride perhaps, but they matched it with courage.

The twelve were now halted while Gunnar felt his way along up there above them in the shadows.

He groaned and called down to them. "I have one foothold. And I can find no more. For twenty feet up the wall is as smooth as ice; and that ledge up above is too rounded to hold my grapple."

"Think of something," a Bron whispered. "My hands will obey me no longer."

"O Thor and Woden," White Owl exclaimed. "To let us go this far and no farther—"

"Wait," Odin called up into the darkness. "Do you have enough of a stance to lower your lariat?"

"I am only holding by one hand. I can lower the thon. But I couldn't lift you, Jack Odin—"

"You won't have to lift me. I'll try the belt that Wolden made."

Ato groaned. "It doesn't always work."

The lariat came coiling down.

Odin knotted it beneath his arms. "Now," he told Gunnar. "When I count three, give a quick yank. Remember—not until I count three—"

"Count, man, count! My arms are not steel—"

And Odin counted: "One—two—three—"

At the count of three he turned the black knob at his belt and pushed himself away from the wall.

There was a sickening feeling of weightlessness. The

moon and the stars became streamers of light as he swung through the air. His body described a semi-circle as he sailed out and up. He struck the parapet high above Gunnar's head just as the surge of power left the belt and weight returned. He lay there for a split second, trying to get his breath, every nerve aching from that quick plunge through a timeless, weightless gulf.

Then he looked about and his spirits soared. Gunnar had flung him to the first rooftop as though he had been a trout.

"Send the men up one by one," Odin called softly. "I'm safe."

One by one Odin pulled them in. And last came Gunnar, his forearms so knotted that the muscles seemed to have been carved there.

From that vantage point, the Tower began to taper. There were so many carvings that the remaining climb was child's play compared to the sheer wall that they had mastered.

Another hundred feet and they pulled themselves onto one of those elaborate balconies. It must have cost a fortune, but that was not their concern. White Owl and Gunnar found a pair of metal doors. There was a wail of complaint as the doors swung inward. They tumbled into a dark room. Gunnar found a switch and turned on a blazing light.

"See, friend Odin," he called out cheerily. "The upper levels of the Treasure House belonged to the Neeblings in the old days. We have not forgotten—"

They were in a corridor, carpeted in a purple velvet pile that must have been fully two inches thick. Gunnar and White Owl led the group until they came to a golden door. Feeling over it, the two dwarfs found a spring. The door opened. Again, Gunnar found a switch and flooded the room before them with light. It was a throne-room. Seated upon a peacock throne was the mummified body of a dwarf-king. A golden mask covered the dead man's face.

"This is the throne-room of Baldar—" Gunnar told them. "Look about you, now. Can you read the golden runes upon the four walls?"

They could not, and the Brons began to fidget. Even Ato was embarrassed. "Then I will read some of the writing," Gunnar exclaimed. "We have been too long silent. The throne-room of Baldar has been sealed too long. Listen—" And he began to read:

"Now, the ship of the Brons arrived upon earth. And the Brons were spent. Also, these were the descendants of soldiers, and they knew nothing of the power that had sped their ship through the gulf of space. They were helpless. Then they found the Neeblings who were rulers of the earth in those days—the Little People Under the Hills, which every race knows, or remembers in their legends. We were of the strain of the Norsemen. The Neeblings were masters of the forge and they lived in caves. Now, lest the Brons be killed by savages, the Neeblings took them in. They studied the ship, and they learned its secrets for they were masters of metalwork. And in time they moved to the caverns below the earth and built them a sun of the ancient magic that they discovered in the ship. And they built them a land, the Brons and the Neeblings. The Neeblings ferreted the old learnings from the ship that the Brons brought with them—for the Brons knew nothing of the power that drove them. And they pledged themselves to share and share alike in the world that they made. They built them a Treasure House and the massive gates that opened upon the floor of the sea. And they stored the ship and other treasures there. This is the story of Baldar, King of the Neeblings and one of the Council. Listen to Baldar's story, for the pledge has been sealed with blood and fire—and the Brons and the Neeblings shall be brothers forever, or the land will be cursed—"

Gunnar's voice ended in a roar of triumph. "We have been patient too long. The Brons have been too arrogant. One by one, the equal rights have disappeared. And now, tonight, the inequalities will end—for I am Gunnar, and I am next in line to Jul, who was killed. And I decree that the inequalities begun so long ago will end tonight—and the Neeblings will be done with the Brons forever—"

Ato took his hand. "You are right, Gunnar. But too many rooms up here have been sealed away and lost. They should have been opened long ago. Even so, none of us helped to shape that injustice. Bear with us a while. I will show you that we can fight by your side, even as we fought in the old days—"

"With you, Ato, we have no quarrel. And I am pledged to fight for Maya, if she is still alive. But the Brons must lose their arrogance—or Opal will be carmined with their blood."

"Let us not fight with each other," Odin urged. "I stand up against all that Grim Hagen represents, Gunnar, but I am not yet convinced that Grim represents all of the Brons."

"And will you stand here quarreling like old women?" White Owl asked. "We came here to fight. Let us find our way to the lower levels and get this over. My sword is still thirsty—"

"We will, little man. We will," Gunnar insisted. "But here is a lesson for all of us to learn. There is much more writing upon the walls. The Brons even forgot their own language and adopted the words of the Neeblings. And then, in their arrogance, they cast the Neeblings aside. And we of the Neeblings let matters pass, for we were pledged by blood and fire. And if our brothers had forgotten, we had not—"

"Will you talk forever!" White Owl exclaimed. "Some day we can tell the old tales by moonlight. But this is a night for fighting—"

"Well, and good, little man." Gunnar shrugged his huge

shoulders. "If it's fighting you want—"

And he led them from Baldar's Throne-Room into a hall, and finally they found a stairway and marched quietly down to the lower levels.

CHAPTER TWELVE

GUNNAR left them in the darkness of the second floor and stole down the stairs for a look at things. Minutes later he came back.

"Grim Hagen and his captains are in the Hall of Triumph," he told them, in rare good humor. "My people built that hall. I wonder if Grim Hagen knows about the doors. They have Maya, Wolden, and at least twenty others captive. A score of soldiers are with them. But most of Hagen's men are near the front of the Tower, awaiting another attack."

"And is that all?" White Owl asked scornfully. "Why, we have been expecting a battle. One side, now, while I go down and exterminate them."

Gunnar stopped him. "Wait, you bloodthirsty little man. There are but twelve of us. If we can surprise them, I think Wolden and his men will help even with their bare hands. But let me tell you about that hall. There are two doors that recede into the wall when they are open. It takes two strong men to open and close them. But just inside the hall there is a statue of a charging saber-tooth. Hidden in the saber-tooth's belly there is a switch that closes and locks those doors. The Hall of Triumph was both a banquet hall and a council chamber in the old days. Grim Hagen and his men are about the banquet table now, listening to words of victory from their captains in Valla and Orthe-Gard. The prisoners are seated below them, guarded by the soldiers. There are four soldiers at the doorway. Also, the doorway is within the view of the man who guards the front of the building. Now, we must swarm down there. The four soldiers must go first. Then, we must go inside. Hold anyone away from me while I get to that saber-tooth statue. Once I find that switch, then Grim Hagen could have a million men outside and it would not matter. We will have only him and his men inside to deal with. Do you understand?"

They checked the plans once more. And then they went down the last stairs, their swords ready.

At the foot of the stairway, Gunnar screamed out the old berserker war cry. They made a rush for four soldiers at the open door. From the front of the building the guards came on the double to stop them.

The four guards who were nearest braced themselves for the attack. A dwarf cast a lariat and drew one toward him. A Bron threw a knife into the throat of another guard. The other two fell back before the rush of the invading twelve.

They were inside the hall now. Soldiers from the front of the Tower were hastening toward them. The two remaining guards went down. Odin and his men turned to stop the onrushing soldiers. Gunnar fell upon his knees beside the gold statue of the saber-tooth, feeling across its middle.

At least a hundred men were at the doorway now. Spears and swords flashed. Odin swung a chair with all his might and it cleared a swathe through the crowd.

Then Gunnar found the switch, and noiselessly the doors closed. One man came through just before they snapped shut. White Owl nearly decapitated him.

Now the soldiers within the hall were advancing. Wolden and the other prisoners flung themselves upon them. Jack Odin caught a glimpse of Maya as Grim Hagen cuffed her to her knees. Then Hagen and his captains came to meet them.

White Owl and Gunnar were screaming the weirdest war cries Odin had ever heard. Grim Hagen and his captains answered. The first wave of Grim Hagen's men was upon them now, and Gunnar swung his broadsword. They went down like wheat. Wolden and his men had grabbed up chairs and anything they could find. There was a bedlam of screams and howls. White Owl was fighting like a wolverine. Small as he was, he was so quick and strong that he had slit the throats of two soldiers before Grim Hagen's men closed about him.

And after that, there was no single event to be remembered. Cries, flashing blades, the smell of fresh blood, these things Jack Odin would recall for the rest of his life. But of the passing of time and the sequence of events, he could remember nothing. The dead and dying slid to the floor. Men cursed, screamed, and prayed. A fallen man slashed at Odin's ankle. And Odin ducked just in time to stop the blade with his own. Then he split the man's skull with one swing of his blade. Over all was the piercing thunder of Gunnar's battle cries.

Gray-haired Wolden was swinging the broken half of a chair while one of Grim Hagen's men was thrusting at him with a razor-sharp blade. Ato was struggling forward, coming to his father's assistance. Then the soldier went down. And there was Maya, her dark hair falling about her shoulders, her eyes blazing. She had buried a knife in the man's ribs. And when he fell at her feet she wiped her forehead with her hand and began to cry.

Behind them, the soldiers were swinging a battering ram against the closed doors. They might as well have used a feather duster.

And then, at last, it was over. None of Grim Hagen's men was left standing.

And Maya was in Odin's arms, her warm lips against his, her body pressed close.

Gunnar cried out to Odin. He had found White Owl

beneath two of Hagen's soldiers.

"Stay here, dearest," Odin said to Maya. "Wait for me—"

"Always," she answered.

They rescued White Owl from the two bodies that were crushing him. The little man had three holes in his chest, and blood was dripping from the corner of his mouth. He grinned when he saw Gunnar. "It was a good fight, eh? A good fight. Hold tight to my arm, Gunnar. I go past the lock of the knitted gates."

And White Owl died.

Tears were streaming from Gunnar's eyes as he straightened the body of his friend. Then he got to his feet.

"Now, where is Grim Hagen? I wish to kill him slowly. Very slowly."

But Grim Hagen was not to be found. They did find an air vent whose steel grill had been slashed open. Evidently, Grim Hagen had slid through the ventilator like a snake when he saw that his battle was lost.

The soldiers who had been battering at the door soon gave up the fight. With no further word from their master they drifted away from the Tower to loot and pillage until finally the re-grouped citizens of Orthe-Gard hunted them down.

But Grim Hagen had vanished into the night.

CHAPTER THIRTEEN

BY THE time the little sun flamed up into light for the new day, the radio reports were turning in Maya's favor. The fighting at Valla had been bloody, and at first her followers had seemed lost. Those who were in favor of the old regime had been driven into the forests. But there they had been joined by dwarfs from the meadowlands. Furthermore, the seamen had stayed loyal to Maya. The only navy that Grim Hagen had mustered was in Orthe-Gard. Now, Maya's sailors held the new-built docks and piers.

Maya's friends renewed their assault. Grim Hagen's troops were in the plight of an army that has used its utmost strength for the first attack. With the onslaught of Maya's troops—steadily enforced by sailors, hunters and ranchers—the resistance of Grim Hagen's men grew weaker and weaker. Toward morning their situation seemed hopeless. They fired the piers once more and made a last stand against the sea. Most of them died there.

Meanwhile, in Orthe-Gard, things went slower but victory loomed closer as the hours passed. Grim Hagen had sunk every ship that might stand in his way. His own navy rained a steady stream of explosives and fireballs upon the town. Wolden and the Scientists managed to repair some huge guns and lugged them to the upper levels of the Treasure House. As soon as morning came, they began to fire—slowly and awkwardly but improving with each shot—until they saw Grim Hagen's flagship go up in smoke. One by one, Grim Hagen's navy was blown apart. The last few ships crept away at their usual slow pace, such an easy target that only six managed to reach the safety of a cloudbank.

The Philosophers had few reinforcements from the rest of their peninsula. There were only a few dwarfs and hunters within the vicinity. However, as the morning passed, the invaders fell one by one. And by twelve o'clock there was only scattered fighting in Orthe-Gard, where looters had holed up in captured houses. Ato and his troops managed to surround each area and dispose of Grim Hagen's men. It was a slow business, but it was sure.

Toward nightfall—or as the people of Opal called it, "Moon-break"—there was no resistance left in the city.

Grim Hagen's conspiracy had failed. But no one had seen Grim Hagen, alive or dead.

During the days that followed, Maya and Odin were in

constant touch with Valla. But, meanwhile, there was a great deal of work to be done in Orthe-Gard. The treasures from the lower levels of the Tower had been pilfered and strewn all the way from there to the docks. Some were never found, but many were restored.

There were hundreds of dead to be buried. Orthe-Gard had suffered heavy losses that night. There were houses and towers to be repaired. And, even more important, the shattered navy had to be brought up from the sea and rebuilt.

"It is a good sound," Gunnar told Maya and Odin, "the sound of the hammer. We thought we had everything done that was needed to be done. But I think when the noise of the hammer dies, a country dies. Or a city. We must not forget this lesson."

Gunnar did consent to attend the council meetings. But most of his time was spent in preparing two huge caskets from the whitest oak for Jul and White Owl. Their bodies were preserved in salt, and they were to go back to Valla in state. Huge caskets for such small men, Odin thought. But Gunnar worked tirelessly with chisel and mall. Those caskets were covered with stout Norse runes and pictures of the old Norse Gods. And the valkyries hovered everywhere to attend to the wishes of Jul and White Owl. Barbarous and beautiful, those caskets, fashioned with all the loving care that Gunnar could give them. Rude when compared to the exact art of the Brons, but the strength of Gunnar flowed into his chisel and these caskets would have been museum pieces in the world above.

Maya sent word for her people to dispatch a fleet to Orthe-Gard. Meanwhile, the work went on. Gunnar replaced old Jul in the council. Temporarily, Ato had been chosen by the survivors to replace Grim Hagen.

There was a deal of old laws being changed. Old men,

wearing heavy spectacles, searched the leather-bound, deckle-edged volumes of the past. And when they found one line that was restrictive to the Neeblings, that line was erased by a new law.

There came a day when the Council and the lesser authorities of Orthe-Gard made a breath-taking climb to the upper levels of the Treasure House. There, with a solemn assemblage about him, Gunnar read the runes upon the walls of the Throne-Room of Baldar.

Maya was crying when he had finished. "And, Gunnar, you and Jul and White Owl stayed faithful to me—after knowing all this?"

"There was the pledge of blood and fire. And, also, princess, we liked you and your father before you."

She kissed him, and Gunnar flushed crimson. "Eh, I liked that," he said. "But no more of this. There is work to be done, and what will my wife Freida say when Gunnar returns from his wanderings and tells of being kissed by the most beautiful girl in the land? She will either say that Gunnar is growing old and lying, or she will whack him one." He chuckled. "Anyway, I tell her. Her and the children. It will be a tale for a family to remember, like the story of mine grandfather catching the giant squid—although one jealous old man swore to the last that grandfather found the squid in a bottle."

The helicopters in the Treasure House were given new motors and were turned over to Gunnar for storage and distribution.

At Maya's request other machines were taken aboard the repaired ships. Valla had been too long without them, she said. Now, perhaps, her people had learned their lesson. A race could make a cult of their strength and endurance long enough. Why throw away the things that their ancestors had mastered?

The repair of Orthe-Gard was nearly completed when the ships from Valla hove into sight.

The return to Valla was uneventful. Wolden, Ato, and a few chosen troops went with them. The Council met for an hour each day. Otherwise, there was little to do except stand by the rail and enjoy the sun and watch the creatures of that teeming sun going about their play and their feeding. The pace of the ships had not been changed, although Odin had learned that this was possible.

"It would be a drain upon the sun," Wolden had advised. "Besides, what would we do with the extra time if we got there in such a hurry?"

The sun was behaving beautifully. For the moment, there seemed to be no worries left in the world of Opal. And with Maya leaning against him at the rail, and the jasmine fragrance of perfumed dark curls in the air, Odin agreed that this was no time for hurrying.

After much secret planning and talks of the future—talks which were invariably interrupted by moments which seemed much more important than the future—Jack Odin and Maya brought the matter of their approaching marriage to the Council.

"I have thought of this question," Wolden answered solidly. "For it has been upon your faces since first we met. Still, in view of our plans, I would advise that the marriage be postponed."

"But, no," Maya exclaimed. "For good or ill, the old law forbids anyone tampering with a marriage."

"True," Wolden answered. "We cannot stop you. But we are staking all our hopes on your mission to the upper world. When the time is right, we will contact them. As you now are, you can meet with them as two representatives of the Council. Married, it might appear to some that you are merely a princess and her consort. Furthermore, if all goes well, the world above will go wild over that approaching marriage. Whatever their faults, they love a lover—"

"He speaks truth, lad," Gunnar advised. "Go up there as a lover. Not as a bridegroom. A flower, a flounder, and a bridegroom—these fade fast enough."

Odin and Maya reluctantly agreed to accept the decision of the Council. Ato hesitated, but voted along with his father and Gunnar.

And so it was agreed—and so it was writ in the journal of the Council—

Then, on a morning when misty rain was falling about them, they sighted the towers of Valla. Rain-washed and free, the city and its beaches, and its emerald forests beyond welcomed their homecoming children.

CHAPTER FOURTEEN

IT IS A matter of timing," said Wolden. "Once you have started on your way to the upper world we will contact the authorities. That will be a moment to stand out in history. In all the years, we have never sent a diplomatic party to the lands above. True, we have gone there. But this, as I see it, must be timed perfectly. You must be met by those in authority. If we let the news out too soon, your arrival will be like a county fair. Every churl for miles around will be there. Some will even be selling hot dogs and peanuts. I have a few recordings of the Floyd Collins incident and the Udall Tornado which would turn your stomach."

He pinched his thin lips in worriment. "It is the most important matter in our history. Our lives may hang in the balance. It is up to us to plan, to think—"

And Maya murmured: "I wonder if they will like my clothes."

Odin started to laugh, but Wolden frowned a warning. "Never laugh at a woman's clothes. Women's clothes have made history—"

"Or Godiva's and Bathsheba's lack of them," Odin retorted. "Honestly, aren't we taking this matter too seriously? Maya and I will have to go up there and do the best we can. Excuse me if I am taking this too lightly, but our trip can't be reduced to a mathematical formula."

Wolden sighed. "But so much depends on the next few days. That world of yours is already overcrowded. And we do have much treasures here. We don't want to end up as the Incas did. Nor do we want to become pawns in international affairs."

"My people are just—" Odin retorted.

But even Gunnar was doubtful. "I was up there, and I had a feeling of gloom about me, as though the Old Worm had finally gnawed through the roots of the tree of Yggdrasil, and the mad squirrel upon its branches was about to run amuck with such mischief that we had never endured before. I have the same feeling now. We are leaving something out of our plans. I wish I felt better about the journey—"

"Nonsense," said Odin. "You crept through alleys like lost dogs when you should have been announcing yourselves at the White House."

"Well, it is all done now," was Gunnar's reply. "And I wish you the best—"

"And we will do our best," Odin promised.

Gunnar looked down at his big hands. "I wish I had got these around Grim Hagen's throat. Then I would feel much better."

Days of preparation went by. Treasures were sorted and stored in the elevator that had brought Odin to the land of Opal. Documents were carefully selected, lest there be any suspicion of fraud. Here was a key to the writings of Crete and there a burned brick that bore Tiglath-Pileser's signature. Photographs, haphazard recordings, pictures of the stars, maps, things from the sea, Spanish coins, and dozens of other treasures. Maya added her wardrobe and the two statuettes. Gunnar tossed in a saber-tooth from a tiger not five days dead and a little package of oat-seeds which were twice as large as any grown in the upper world. "Maybe simple men will understand these things better than the writings," he explained.

The day for Odin and Maya's departure from Opal finally arrived. The door to the once-forbidden elevator was open. For once, the people of Valla forgot their inclination to leave the other fellow alone and turned out for a holiday of bunting, bands and flags. The little sun held steady above them. And the breezes from the land where it was always June were cool and fragrant.

Escorted by Wolden, Ato, and Gunnar the two were paraded from the town. Along the shell paved road. Up the long, wide stairway that was flecked with gold. The throng pressed close behind them, cheering them on.

Now they stood at the door to the shaft.

"It is ready," Wolden explained. "We have installed automatic controls. It is stocked with oxygen and food. The trip upward will be much longer, but you will not have to watch the machines. I checked them yesterday and these guards have not been away from the door. There, now…in you go. The best of luck to you, and the best of luck to your mission—"

He whispered softly in Odin's ear. "I have just received a report that the sun has lost more of its energy. Hurry, man, lest it start flickering. Some of these people still believe in omens—"

The crowd was cheering and closing in, almost shoving Wolden and his companions into the elevator along with

Odin and Maya.

They stood there for a moment, waving their farewells.

"Now," Odin heard Wolden cry out. "Make ready."

Slowly the door to the elevator began to close. The bands played louder. Odin and Maya waved once more.

And then it happened.

All was confusion on the steps before the elevator shaft. A knife flashed in the sun. Someone screamed. A skillfully thrown lariat settled about Maya's shoulders. Odin clutched at her and missed. And Maya was drawn through the closing door. She cried out once in pain and fear. Soldiers were ripping at each other with flashing blades. Odin saw Gunnar's broadsword go up and down and heard his shrill war cry as he fought his way to Maya's side.

He struggled with the door. It was too narrow now for him to get through. He tried to force it back—struggled with it until it was relentlessly closing upon his fingers.

He lost his grip and fell back. There was a roaring of old, stout machines in his ears. Then slowly the elevator moved upward. It gained speed and the noise of the machines dwined to a faint humming.

He tried to remember the controls that Gunnar and Maya had worked. But they were gone. Wolden, thinking to help, had ruined him with those automatic controls.

There was a radio within the room. He turned it on, but got only silence. The radio was dead.

Everything had been tampered with. Not half the treasures they had stored remained. Now, to make matters worse, the yellow light above his head began to flicker. Finally it went out, leaving him in pitch darkness. And still the elevator went slowly up. Once it ground to a halt—moved sideways like a crab—and then roared again as it moved aloft.

At long last he found food and water. The thought came

to him that perhaps it had been poisoned. But he was feeling so low that he did not care. He ate and drank. Then he sat there in the darkness, promising himself what he would do to Grim Hagen if he ever caught him.

Surely this was Grim Hagen's work. Those soldiers that Wolden had trusted. Grim Hagen's men, doubtless. For if they were not, then Wolden was the traitor—and Wolden had been too worried, too sincere, too friendly to do a thing like this.

Then, sitting there in the darkness, he heard the tick-tick-ticking of a clock. He and Maya carried watches; they did not require a clock.

His last matches went to find the source of that ticking which seemed to be growing louder all the while. They were wasted. There was no clock in sight, though he searched everywhere—

He sat there in the darkness now, and the ticking increased in loudness almost to hammer blows. A time bomb, he decided. Well, Grim Hagen had been good at planning. What did it matter now—?

But soon it appeared that Grim Hagen had taken no chances. The air was growing heavy. Something had gone wrong with the oxygen controls.

Odin went to his knees. After breathing became uncomfortable there, he lay flat upon his belly. The air was cool and fresh for a few minutes. Then it too became heavy.

The blackness burgeoned into flame. Here was a sun that was flickering out, and here was a world of emerald and turquoise where it was always June. And there, standing like a goddess was a golden girl with golden eyes who held her arms out to him. The sun and the world became one vast jewel of flame. And standing there in the center of the jewel, a tiptoed silhouette reaching out to him, was the golden girl. Then the jewel burst into a million sparks. They sailed through the sky—hurrying to join the drift of suns. Tiny bubbles of light fled away from him and on each sparkling bubble was a golden girl who held her arms out to him and called farewell.

Then there was nothing but blackness.

When he awoke, good cool air was flowing across his face. The elevator had stopped. The door had opened. Out there was a glimpse of a blue sky and a few tattered mesquites. The elevator had thrust its way up through rocks and clay and had come to rest.

He listened. A bird was singing—a sad, plaintive song, as though it had lost its mate.

But there was another sound. Nearer. He got to his knees and listened again.

"Tick. Tick. Tick."

And he remembered the sound that had tortured him all the way through the dark trip upward.

Odin got to his feet and leaped through the doorway. He fell over and over as he rolled down the incline of clay and rocks that the elevator had shoved upward. Then he got to his feet and ran a few more steps. Ran until he could go no farther. Lord, he was weak, he thought. And how could a man tear the world apart to find Maya when he was as weak as this?

The fall saved him.

Behind him the elevator, the rocks and the clay melted into one fiery blast.

Stones rained about him. Steel whistled over his head.

He dug into the ground, while the sound of the explosion tore at his ears and the flame scorched the shirt from his back.

Minutes later, when he got to his feet again, there was no sound anywhere. The bird had either been killed or had flown away. His back and arms were blistered. One shoe-sole flopped as he limped away.

Dazed and hurt, he stumbled along. A walking scarecrow. Now and then he stopped to rest, but he kept getting up and going on. He fell against a mesquite once and it lashed him with its thorns. But he kept going on until he found an old cattle trail. He went along it until he came to a hard-baked, rutted road. And this he followed until he came to a paved highway that went straight across a land that was made up of little rolling hills. It must be springtime up here, he thought. For not far away was a field of blue bonnets.

He staggered along the gray highway for a few more minutes. Then he fell again, struggled up only to fall once more.

A passing motorist found him and carried him on to the nearest town.

CHAPTER FIFTEEN

JACK ODIN knew little of the happenings of the next two weeks. He was a patient in the charity ward of a Texas hospital. They treated him well, these Texans, though the county sheriff asked him countless questions toward the last. The sheriff and even the Ranger who came to see him were convinced, apparently, that he had been tortured by gangsters and thrown out of a car.

He was shown a map of the vicinity where he had been found, and learned that most of the land in that area consisted of marginal ranches that had been abandoned during the drought. No one had heard an explosion.

They had been so hospitable to him that he did not know what to say. Finally, in desperation, he told the truth to the sheriff. The next day a doctor from Austin called upon Odin and listened to the tale. The second day he returned—and the third, making notes all the while.

On the fourth day, the doctor tried to talk to him.

"We have sent some telegrams and have made a few long-distance calls. You are Doctor Jack Odin. That much we know. We found a veteran in the next county who remembers you from Korea. You patched him up. Now, it is my theory, doctor, that you simply cracked up as a result of the war and the troubles that you had in Maryland. These stories of the land of Opal. Why, man, people have been looking for a world where it is always June since Eden was lost. And Maya! Even the name is a psychological phenomenon. As for the dwarfish Norsemen and their mythology—why, all mythology is sound. Metaphorically, at least, there has always been a tree of Yggdrasil, with its branches in heaven and its roots in hell. And the worm of death has always gnawed at it. The squirrel of mischief or 'happenstance' has always darted from branch to branch. For the affairs of men are never settled. Now, be reasonable, Doctor Odin, you simply blacked out and went wandering across the country. You fell among thieves. They took your money and identifications and left you for dead on the highway. You were badly burned, as from a blowtorch. Or lighter fluid blazing across your back might have caused those injuries. You don't remember any of them? The sadists! Don't worry...we'll catch them yet."

A Texan to the last, the doctor was certain that no criminal, sane or mad, could escape the Rangers.

In vain, Odin swore that his story was true, and there were no fiends that had tortured and robbed him. There was a certain hell's spawn by the name of Grim Hagen who he intended to find if it took the rest of his days.

But it was no use. They released him when his old attorney from Washington came out to get him. Noland, who had been his father's friend, was a very successful lawyer indeed, but he had not been west of the Potomac in forty years. He had already convinced himself that Jack Odin and all Texans were mad.

So after writing some substantial checks to the men and the hospital that had saved him, Jack Odin came back to Washington and Baltimore.

The next two weeks were mere repetitions of the last days in the little Texas hospital. Using his father's name, Odin went to some Government officials who refused to believe one word of his story.

At last, Odin wished them a fond goodbye. Then he made arrangements to open up a research office in Washington. He found some rooms above several tiny little stores on K Street. They were not the best, but he was not interested in business or a career. The men he hired were trained in research. Some had degrees in Oceanography and Geophysics. He set them to work in the Smithsonian and the labyrinths of the Congressional Library.

Each Friday, they went over the week's findings. Things were shaping up. The evidence in his favor was growing.

Given six more months and a staff such as this, he was sure that he could prove his story and the existence of the world of Opal. Fortunately, there was plenty of money to meet expenses.

Then came the news that closed the offices. At first, it was just a tiny squib from the Houston Press which told of a swirling little fountain of steam spouting out of the Gulf some fifty miles to the south of Galveston. Two passing ships had sighted it. The next day there was a report that the geyser of steam had grown larger and the waters about it appeared to be smoldering.

On the third day the steam was forgotten. The waters of the Gulf had begun to recede, rapidly. A luxury fishing boat came in from the Dry Tortugas with ailing passengers and crew. The ship was radioactive. And far out in the Gulf there was a play of lights as though the aurora of the North had fled southward.

The waters receded more. In the long run, the states along the Gulf Coast benefited from the events that followed. But for several days the cities and the beaches faced unleashed fury.

The Gulf continued to recede, and then with little warning burst into a Tidal Wave. The main force appeared to be centered upon Galveston. But the city had been caught by disaster before and was prepared. Storms of deadly violence raged all over the Gulf, and up and down the coast. Survivors reported that their ships had simply fallen apart. Miami faced the worst hurricane of its history. As for the planes that were flying those waters that grim, gray morning, not one survived.

It was the morning of October 1st. The Gulf states were having so much trouble with the storms, and even reporters and photographers along the coast were so busily hunting through the wreckage, that no one knows the truth of the happenings that occurred.

It is certain that the Air Force and the Coast Guard kept records and made reports accordingly. But those reports have not yet been released.

Out where the little geyser of steam had first appeared, the smoldering sea suddenly turned into flame as though an underwater volcano had just been born. The flame continued, spouting toward the sky in every color of the rainbow.

The flame rose higher. The Tidal Wave was at its worst. And then, quite leisurely, an hourglass shape shook itself from the waters. It went straight upward. As one man said: "It looked like a little sun with dozens of tiny moons coiling up and down and around. A perfect hourglass with the sun in the very center—"

Others referred to it as an enormous X, slightly bulged at the intersection of the arms.

Once out of the sea the shape began to pick up speed. And the strangest phenomenon of all was that as it climbed higher into the sky it seemed to grow.

A seaman, who at the time was clinging to a shattered boat with the colored water beating around him, later said: "I was the nearest one to it, I think. When it left the water, it was like being struck by an electric eel. But that wasn't the worst shock. It was the way it grew. Five miles up, it looked much larger than when I first saw it. And as it went up and up it was still growing."

These are the reports of the first happenings of that gray, stormy morning. Most of them have been howled down, as tales born of terror and superstition during the worst storm of the century.

But they persist.

Meanwhile, the glowing shape went higher, always increasing speed, always growing.

It was miles into the air now and nearly a mile across. Watchers from other states saw it as a soaring rocket—or, as many said, "a flying saucer of blazing force."

Its speed suddenly diminished, although the whirling moons flashed brighter and the central core of the thing was noticeably growing. Almost motionless in the sky it dropped something down. A gleaming yo-yo on a silver string. A golden spider climbing down a glistening thread. These words have been used to describe it. And yet there are some who swear they saw nothing.

The ball at the end of the glistening thread came near the waters. It began to grow. It sucked up a whirling sphere.

And, still drawing its stores from the sea and still growing, the craft up there in the ionosphere flashed two dazzling shafts of light down upon the earth. One burst high above Washington. The other high above Moscow. As though it played no favorites. These blazed high above the cities, and they must have been warning blasts, surely. For the thermometers in each city climbed to 110^0. The barometers dropped low, as though all pressure were being burned away from the two areas.

Then the whirling sphere of water was drawn upward, freezing as it went. Trailing the globe behind it like a pinnace, the growing hourglass of central light and coiling moons darted upward at a pace that defied the astronomers. Still growing, they vanished or melted into space. Before they faded they filled one-twelfth of the sky. A glowing mist that trailed away, leaving men to squabble over the cause of a storm. Or the phenomenon that a storm can create.

Storms and cyclones followed the two blasts. The seas of the world were troubled.

In time, the Gulf quieted. The Gulf States—Texas especially—found themselves the happy owners of miles and miles of additional land. Before the mud had dried, oil seepage was glistening in the sun, and drilling crews were moving in.

Back in Washington, when the news had subsided, Doctor Jack Odin and his men made a last desperate attempt to correlate the events of those three days. There was too much confusion. There were too many reports. Some were being studied by the authorities and could not be released at the present time.

Time was growing short. Odin gave each man an extra check and closed his office. Then he deposited six thousand dollars to the credit of a Geophysicist who had a talent for questions, and instructed him to devote a year to the events of October 1st.

Just before Odin snapped out the light in his office, at the close of that last wearisome day, he scrawled a few lines as a postscript to the notes he had been preparing:

And like a soul belated,
In hell and heaven unmated,
By cloud and mist abated
Comes out of darkness morn.

Then, taking his notes with him, he closed his tiny offices on K Street forever.

No one in Washington or Baltimore saw Doctor Jack Odin after that night.

The general belief is that he had another spell of amnesia and went wandering once more.

Some distant cousins are fighting furiously over his estate.

CHAPTER SIXTEEN

ON THE night when this adventure began, you may remember that Jack Odin was writing a letter to a friend in Kansas.

I am that friend.

He never finished the letter. But several months ago I did hear from him. The postman delivered a sealed bundle of papers to me that had been mailed first class from Georgetown, Texas. Aside from the postmark, there was no return address.

I unsealed the package and found page after page of notes, carefully numbered, but in places so terse and so hastily written that the narrative was difficult to follow. Odin is one of those writers who can condense a page into a sentence and a sentence into a comma.

They became more incoherent toward the last, as though the writer was shaken by grief and agitation.

"Dear Joe:" his letter began, "you always liked to monkey around with words. Maybe you can piece these pages together. At any rate they will explain why I haven't written for so long."

The balance of his letter contained so many personal remarks, mingled with his plans and what had happened to him since his disappearance from Washington, that I will not copy it. Instead, I have sifted out the last lines of his narrative—just as I have pieced the preceding chapters together from the notes that he sent me. "For," as he said toward the close of his letter, "time is growing short and the tale is almost ended."

It was the doctor from Austin who brought Jack back to Texas. A kindly man, he had written Jack a long letter and enclosed a clipping from a local paper.

Now, it seems that a certain rancher by the name of Jim Keefe had been set upon by three murderous little men one moonlit night. Keefe, who lived some twenty miles northeast of Fredericksburg, had been in Austin on business. The business attended to, and being mighty dry, he had spent some time at a local bar. Then, in spite of all the warnings of Safety Commissions and the law, he had purchased a bottle and, putting it on the seat beside him, had steered an unsteady course for home. At last, when he closed his gate behind him and started his pickup over the rutted trail that led to his ranch house, he was very unsteady indeed. He stopped the car and took another drink. There was a full moon out that night—or maybe two of them but Keefe had never been known to see things before.

Keefe sat there for a few minutes with the night wind blowing in his face, and feeling much better, when he saw three figures on the crest of a knoll nearby. They were gaunt and bent. They wore tight fitting, laced jackets, and on their heads each had a peaked cap into which a feather was thrust at a jaunty angle. Each figure carried a bundle over his shoulder. And the largest of the three carried something else. A slaughtered calf. Now, what Texan would stand for that!

Taking a jack-handle from his car, Keefe advanced to meet the three gnarled men. Yelling a battle cry worthy of San Jacinto, he ran toward them, waving his weapon aloft.

They waited. As he drew nearer Keefe saw that all of them were dwarfish, although the one who carried the calf so easily was larger than the other two. All were dressed in a strange fashion.

"You rustling varmints," Keefe yelled, "I'll clobber you—" And he rushed at them, swinging the jack-handle.

Suddenly the largest of the dwarfs let the calf fall from his shoulders. He was wearing a huge broadsword that was slung across his back. The carcass of the calf had hidden it before. With a battle cry that nearly froze Keefe's blood, the little man unsheathed the sword and rushed at the rancher. Had Keefe not been a bit unsteady on his feet, the first blow would have decapitated him.

As it was he slipped nearly to his knees and the broadsword whistled over his head.

The two smaller dwarfs were also advancing.

Keefe righted himself and retreated.

The dwarfs did not follow.

The next day Keefe took his story to the local authorities. Some remembered how thirsty a rancher can get when he comes to town. However, there was an investigation. The only proof of Keefe's story was a bloody spot nearby where unmistakably a calf had been slaughtered.

The doctor's point in writing the letter was convincing to anyone except Odin. The incident proved that thieves were in the vicinity. The thieves were dwarfs and murderous. This, according to the doctor, completed the case of Odin's hiatus. He had picked up the dwarfs somewhere. They had tortured and robbed him, leaving him for dead on the highway. That explained the "dreams" of the little men.

But to Odin it meant that some of the dwarfs had come up from the world of Opal. The largest dwarf with the huge sword. Could that be Gunnar?

All along, his research had pointed more and more to the vicinity of Longhorn Caverns, near Georgetown. He hurried to that city and immediately hired a taxi for side-excursions to the Caverns. He was disappointed. They were closed by a heavy grill. A good-natured, talkative guide took him on a short tour of the labyrinths—the parts that were lighted with electric bulbs. He saw Sam Bass' huge footprint and other formations that might have interested him in other days. But now he was interested in those unexplored pitch-black passages that led away from the tourists' paths. The guide would allow no venturing. Jack Odin went back to Georgetown with the feeling that short of an order from the Governor of Texas he would never explore the Caverns from that entrance.

The next day, he and his taxi-man started out to find Jim Keefe. It took nearly all day, for Jim's ranch was in a lonely spot off the known roads.

Keefe told him the story, now and then making a few remarks as to the ancestry of the men who had laughed at his tale of the dwarfs.

"But what became of them?" Odin asked cautiously, "Have you any idea?"

"Of course, I have. I told the sheriff. He wouldn't even listen. They're hid out in the Hole."

"The Hole?"

"Sure. A hole about six feet across that goes straight down for maybe eight feet and then angles off, and then goes on down again. Dark as pitch. I lost a calf there once, and I've kept it fenced off ever since. A spook place. Those varmints have got away. And, somehow, they looked like critters that would be housed up in such a place. Reminded me of a tale that my grandma used to tell—"

Keefe was on the fringe of bankruptcy, and a check immediately convinced him that Jack Odin was an explorer and should be given permission to investigate the Hole.

Odin went back to Georgetown. He finished his letter and mailed it and the package to me. Then he purchased some food, a high-powered rifle, and some other things. Even the man at the sporting goods store thought that a case of ammunition was a bit too much for a beginner.

Once more the taxi went back to Jim Keefe's place. Odin unloaded his supplies and gave the driver a hundred-dollar bill. Jim Keefe was not there. When he came back, he wrote me later, "the man was gone."

As far as I know, the taxi-driver was the last person to see Jack Odin. I can imagine Jack lugging his things, including a long coil of rope, to that spooky place which Keefe called "The Hole." The hot Texas day would not have bothered him, for he was a strong man.

This much I can imagine. For the last line added to his letter just before he mailed it that day in Georgetown reads:

I'm going back.

THE END

If you've enjoyed this book, you will not want to miss these terrific titles…

ARMCHAIR SCI-FI & HORROR DOUBLE NOVELS, $12.95 each

D-1 **THE GALAXY RAIDERS** by William P. McGivern
SPACE STATION #1 by Frank Belknap Long

D-2 **THE PROGRAMMED PEOPLE** by Jack Sharkey
SLAVES OF THE CRYSTAL BRAIN by William Carter Sawtelle

D-3 **YOU'RE ALL ALONE** by Fritz Leiber
THE LIQUID MAN by Bernard C. Gilford

D-4 **CITADEL OF THE STAR LORDS** by Edmond Hamilton
VOYAGE TO ETERNITY by Milton Lesser

D-5 **IRON MEN OF VENUS** by Don Wilcox
THE MAN WITH ABSOLUTE MOTION by Noel Loomis

D-6 **WHO SOWS THE WIND...** by Rog Phillips
THE PUZZLE PLANET by Robert A. W. Lowndes

D-7 **PLANET OF DREAD** by Murray Leinster
TWICE UPON A TIME by Charles L. Fontenay

D-8 **THE TERROR OUT OF SPACE** by Dwight V. Swain
QUEST OF THE GOLDEN APE by Ivar Jorgensen and Adam Chase

D-9 **SECRET OF MARRACOTT DEEP** by Henry Slesar
PAWN OF THE BLACK FLEET by Mark Clifton.

D-10 **BEYOND THE RINGS OF SATURN** by Robert Moore Williams
A MAN OBSESSED by Alan E. Nourse

ARMCHAIR SCIENCE FICTION CLASSICS, $12.95 each

C-1 **THE GREEN MAN**
by Harold M. Sherman

C-2 **A TRACE OF MEMORY**
By Keith Laumer

C-3 **INTO PLUTONIAN DEPTHS**
by Stanton A. Coblentz

ARMCHAIR MASTERS OF SCIENCE FICTION SERIES, $16.95 each

M-1 **MASTERS OF SCIENCE FICTION, Vol. One**
Bryce Walton—"Dark of the Moon" and other tales

M-2 **MASTERS OF SCIENCE FICTION, Vol. Two**
Jerome Bixby—"One Way Street" and other tales